Advance Praise

"...full of wonderful surprises and weirdn   ;
for Jeremy C. Shipp's earlier works now. I
—John R. Little, Bram Stoker winning author of *Miranda* and *The Gray Zone*

"One of the most original and entertaining books I've read in a long time...The writing is crisp and fast-paced."—Daniel G. Keohane, author of *Solomon's Grave*

"...Shipp's one of a kind voice leads us through an ever-twisting ride inside the netherverse of the mind."—John Palisano

"...delivers a fun ride of mystery and fear mixed in with lashings of dark humor and weird scenes featuring some strange people."—MPN SIMS, co-author of *Department 18*

"*Cursed* is beyond any other bizarre, twisted story I've ever read. I've never enjoyed being slapped so much before."—Jodi Lee, *The New Bedlam Project*

"*Cursed* is: A punch to the back of the head by a six-foot pink bunny. It hurts at first, but then the Vicodin and Jim Beam kick in."—L.L. Soares, author of *In Sickness*

"...a provocative, intense story that distorts the very fabric of fiction."
—Amy Grech, author of *Apple of My Eye* and *Blanket of White*

"...a delightful, quirky read. Shipp keeps you guessing and turning pages."
—Louise Bohmer, author of *The Black Act*

"...alarmingly bizarre, full of odd angles and satirical wit...[Shipp] writes like an outlaw, with an utterly unique voice hellbent on cutting his own path."
—Joe McKinney, author of *Dead City*, *Quarantined*, and *Resistance*

"By turns, this witty, horrific and poignant book dazzles and astounds the reader. This is an unforgettable work—a must read you'll savor long after the final page."—Lisa Mannetti, Bram Stoker Award winning author of *The Gentling Box*

"Fun, weird stuff with writing so sharp and wry, it'll make you want to slap your mama!"— Michael Louis Calvillo, Bram Stoker Nominated author of *I Will Rise* and *As Fate Would Have It*

Laura,
From one word wrangler
to another.

Jeremy C. Shipp

Cursed

Jeremy C. Shipp

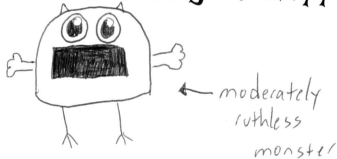

← moderately
ruthless
monster

**RAW DOG
SCREAMING
PRESS**

Published by Raw Dog Screaming Press
Hyattsville, MD

First Edition

Cover and Book Design: John Lawson
Cover Images © 2009 Jupiterimages Corporation

Printed in the United States of America

ISBN 978-1-933293-87-5

Library of Congress Control Number: 2009930320

www.RawDogScreaming.com

For Lisa

Also by Jeremy C. Shipp

Novels
Vacation

Collected Fiction
Sheep and Wolves

#12

THERE ARE 3 ways I can see this night ending:

1. A burglar breaks in and swipes whatever valuables he can find. Basically, that means the Playstation and the pyramid of HBO box sets in the corner. He ends up assaulting me for wasting his time.

2. I get attacked by the ghost of Mario Martinez, the man who was murdered here 30 years ago. The murderer shot him for less than a mound of DVDs. Just one paycheck. And the killer was never caught. The only reason I know all this is because my roommate's aunt is a policewoman and she looked into the homicide for him. Because he begged. Gordon's morbid that way.

3. Someone rings the doorbell and wants to talk.

I think I'd prefer 2, but 3 it is.

Tonight it's Nadia.

I'm not surprised. I'm also not looking forward to this one.

"Can we talk?" she says, and steps through the threshold, arms crossed.

"I actually have a date," I say. "If I don't leave now, I'm gonna be late." I didn't mean for that to rhyme. I feel stupid already.

"This is important," she says, on my couch. She's talking to the spot where she wants me to sit. Like I'm already there.

"Couldn't we do this on the phone? Tomorrow?"

"This is too important for the phone."

I sigh. "I see."

"I drove all the way out here to talk to you. Thirty minutes. The least you can do is give me a minute of your time."

The least I can do is scramble out the door, the building, and hide behind a garbage bin until she goes away. But that hasn't worked for me yet.

"Fine," I say.

Since I don't join her on the couch where I obviously belong, she approaches me. She's more than my sister right now, even if she doesn't know it. She's my past catching up to me.

She's #12.

"Look," she says, and when Nadia says, "Look," what she means is, "I know how to fix all your problems if you just shut up and listen to me for once."

"This morning, Greg and I were sitting on the couch," she says. "We were watching Svetlana play with a little toy xylophone. Me and Greg, you know we've been married for seven years. Out of the blue, on that couch, he held my hand. That little thing, combined with every other wonderful little thing in my life, flooded into me like…well, I don't know what it was like. It was like nothing else. I was this close to pure joy." And she holds her index fingers side by side, in front of her nose.

"Congratulations," I say. She probably thinks I'm being sarcastic. Maybe I even sound sarcastic. But I'm happy for her.

"The point is," she says. "I couldn't reach that pure joy, because of you."

And that little thing, combined with every other little thing she's ever said to me, almost floods out of me in tears. Instead, I say, I crackle, "Thanks."

"I didn't mean it that way." She puts a hand on my shoulder. A move I'm sure she learned from *Full House* or some other TV show back in the 80s. "I just…I mean, I think you should go to church."

"I thought we save this conversation for Christmas. It's only June."

"This is different." She crosses her arms again, blocking her heart. "I realized, during that moment on the couch with Greg, that I'll never be able to feel completely happy. Not now. Not ever. Not even in heaven."

I take this moment to glance at the mole on my left wrist. Sure enough, it's still there.

"How are we supposed to enjoy ourselves up there?" she says. "Knowing that you're below us, trapped for eternity, going through god-knows-what?"

"I'm sure you'll manage somehow."

"I'm serious, Nicholas. This isn't only your life that you're messing with. We're connected. We're all connected." She interlaces her fingers, in front of my nose.

I can't think of anything else to say but, "I'll be fine."

At that, her fingers disconnect in an instant, and she slaps me. She slaps me hard. But it's not really me she's attacking. She's fighting her own fears and doubts, and that's what I tell myself when I touch my throbbing cheek.

"Oh," she says. She looks at me with those I-don't-know-what-got-into-me eyes. And I want to tell her exactly what it is.

Instead, I put a hand on her shoulder, and say, crackle, "I'm fine."

#13

CICELY'S BACK.

My face burns a little, but she's not my girlfriend. She's not even a friend, really. I know her favorite kind of apple and peach. I don't know her last name

During a turn, her cart swerves too far and smacks a ledge of bread.

"God!" Cicely says. There's panic in her voice that I'm sure has nothing to do with bread.

"Damn defective carts," I say, closing in. "I could go find you a new one."

"Nicholas," she says, not smiling for once. "The cart's fine, hon. I'm the defective one."

I laugh, because I always feel like laughing when I'm around Cicely. If she told me her cat died, I might laugh on accident. Then I notice the tennis ball in her right hand. I force myself to look away.

"I missed you last week," I say. I didn't mean to sound so sincere. So small.

Now she smiles. And with a smile like that, she can't be #13.

"I'm sorry I missed it," she says. "I was busy being kidnapped by little green men."

"I should've known."

"Luckily, I annoyed their scientists so much they let me go. It turns out aliens despise show tunes. "Brigadoon" especially."

I laugh. The world is right in the supermarket again.

"Shall we shop?" she says.

We shop.

Cicely grips the cart with her left hand, and presses the tennis ball in her right hand against the handle. She can hardly control the cart. She's sweating. Yet she doesn't put the ball away in her pastel rainbow of a purse.

Maybe she really likes tennis. Maybe this is a sort of physical therapy. I don't know.

What I do know is her List.

I know:

1. 4 organic Granny Smith apples. And she'll say something like, "A little known fact. Apples not only keep away doctors, but flesh-eating zombies. McIntosh don't work though. Don't ask me why."

2. 3 organic yellow peaches. And she'll say, "When I was a girl, I was hated by peaches. We managed to work things out when I was 15. I'm glad we did."

I know the rest.

Or I thought I did.

Cicely's List is different today, completely different, and I feel disoriented.

1. 6 organic Golden Delicious.

2. 1 scoop of walnuts.

3. Some leafy green vegetable. I feel too dizzy to notice what kind.

"You OK?" she says, still sweating like crazy.

"I'm fine," I say, small.

She sets down the cantaloupe, one-handed. "I wasn't really kidnapped by aliens."

"A more cynical person probably would have doubted you," I say. "As it is, I feel betrayed." I try to smile.

"My husband left me."

I'm careful not to laugh. "I'm sorry, Cicely."

I didn't know she was married.

"John wasn't right for me," she says. "I'm an African goddess. He didn't treat me like an African goddess. You can see how that could be a problem."

"Yeah," I say, not laughing.

"Now that he's gone, I feel stupid I stayed with him for so long. I'm 46 years old, for god's sake."

"You're not stupid. You're really…good." I want to bury myself in potatoes.

"Thanks, hon. Oh! Mangos. I'll be right back." She speeds away.

And I look back after her.

What I thought was Cicely's List all this time, wasn't. It was John's.
I watch her hair and only notice that I'm pushing my cart when I hit something.

"Shit!" I say. The panic in my voice has almost everything to do with the little girl I knocked over.

Time for #13.

#14

MY PRESENT TO-MAKE list:

    1. Winged hippo.

    2. Dental drill.

    3. Another Elvis.

Right now, I'm using a chopstick to turn the little hippo legs inside out. I count every leg.

By the time I reach 4, Gordon's inside and undoing Meta's harness. Meta, his Labradoodle.

"Where are you?" Gordon says.

"Here," I say.

Gordon walks over with the harness. "The sign on here, it says something to the effect of 'Do not pet my fucking guide dog,' right?"

"Right," I say.

"It's every fucking day." He hangs the harness on the wall. "People are either inconsiderate or just plain stupid."

"Yeah."

He sits on the couch. "This old lady started petting her today, and I was Mr. Polite. 'Please stop, ma'am. I'd appreciate it if you asked me first before doing that.' But she kept on petting her and I had to walk away before she'd stop. Then there was this guy who barked at her when we were crossing the street. And you know Meta. She's got major ADD. I don't know what people are thinking."

"Sorry," I say. On behalf of all the sighted people in the world, maybe.

He sighs. "No, I'm sorry, Nick. You were here, being all zen and artistic. Then I come in and fuck everything up like the thoughtless assholes I was talking about."

"There's no zen and there's no art. I make stuffed animals."

"Customized plush art. Don't sell yourself short."

"Shut up." I'm ready to load up the hippo, but realize I'm out of polyfil. I'm usually more organized than this. I stretch and join Gordon on the couch. "You'll like this. A woman placed an order today. She wants a bride holding the groom's head. His severed head. She's gonna mail me a photo of the couple to use as a model." I forgot to add this one to my to-make list.

"Some people are weird."

"Coming from a guy obsessed with murderers."

"I'm intrigued by the psychology of violence. Now you're selling me short."

"Sorry."

"My favorite still has to be the head with the open skull. All the penises sticking out of his brain like flowers in a flowerpot. Now that was art."

"You need help."

"I need food." He walks away.

I glance around the living room for a while, for no reason at all. Then I search my pocket for this week's to-do list. I can't find it.

I can't think.

I can, but all I can think about is #14, and I need to do something about it.

I find Gordon in the kitchen, eating leftovers.

"Aren't those mine?" I say.

"You ate yours already. Remember?"

He's right. "Shit. I'm losing it." I didn't mean to sound so alarmed. So loud.

"It's just leftovers, Nick."

"I need you to help me with an experiment."

"Yeah?"

"Stay with me in my room tonight. No one in or out. We'll have to secure the door. It'll only be until midnight."

Gordon exhales hard out his nose. A laugh. "Don't get me wrong. I'm interested, very interested, in what the hell's going on with you, but I have plans tonight. You know, the good kind."

"I'll pay you. I have $114 in my wallet right now."

"I don't know. You make strange whimpering sounds in your sleep. It freaks me out."

"I won't sleep then."

Another hard puff out the nose.

Sure, I'm asleep by 10 every night, but not tonight. If my routine's going to fall apart, at least I can make it crumble on my own terms.

"Alright," Gordon says. And he's more than my roommate right now, even if he doesn't know it. He's my future.

So, to secure the perimeter:

1. Barricade the door with my dresser.

2. Test the bars on the window. Make sure nothing's loose.

3. Check the closet for monsters or otherwise.

4. Check under the bed.

"So…what exactly's supposed to happen here?" Gordon says.

My face burns.

"Well?" he says.

He's part of this now. I might as well tell him.

"You're gonna slap me," I say. "Unless someone breaks through the door and slaps me. Or the window. Or Meta slaps me. But I'm not sure if dogs count."

"Jesus fuck," Gordon says. "Why would I slap you?"

"I don't know."

"Why would anyone slap you? You're the nicest guy I know."

"I'm not nice."

"Yeah, you are."

I sigh.

And Gordon drops the subject. A move I'm sure he didn't learn from an 80s TV show.

Before long, Gordon's asleep on my bed, snug in his sleeping bag, with Meta curled up beside him. They're both snoring. If I weren't frowning so hard, I might smile.

Instead, I'm sitting at my desk, watching the clock.

The time's 11:35.

25 more minutes, and I can breathe again.

I hear something scratching at the door. I shiver. I think:

    1. Mario Martinez

    2. The man who killed Mario Martinez.

But I stand, and it's Meta clawing at the dresser.

Gordon walks into my nightstand. "Fuck," he says. "Forgot what room I'm in."

"Sorry," I say.

"Help me move the dresser."

"There's still time left. 24 minutes."

"Meta needs to pee."

"Let her pee on the floor."

"She doesn't want to pee on the floor, Nick."

"I don't care."

"This is fucking crazy." He pushes on the dresser.

And Gordon's one of the last people in the world I'd imagine slapping me. The last people:

    1. Gordon.

    2. Cicely.

    3. Sol, my step-father.

I need to know what's happening to me. I need to know if one of these people would cross the line if my destiny demanded it.

So I pull Gordon away from the dresser.

"Let me go!" he says.

I don't.

And he slaps me.

#14. And that little number, combined with every other little number that led up to it, makes me sick to my stomach.

Gordon touches his hand to his cheek, like he feels my pain. Maybe he does. "I'm sorry," he says. "I can't believe I just did that."

"I'm sorry I grabbed you," I say.

"I shouldn't've reacted that way."

"It's not your fault."

"Yes, it is."

"Let's move the dresser."

We do.

"Don't sleep yet," he says. "I want to talk to you when we get back."

He gets to work putting on Meta's harness, and she already peed on the floor. I don't tell him. I sit on the couch in the living room, waiting, staring at Gordon's spot next to me. Like he's already there.

When he is, I say, "It really wasn't your fault."

"It really was," he says. "I have this thing about being touched. I freaked out. I shouldn't've punched you."

"You slapped me."

"Whatever. I'm sorry."

"Stop saying that. You were the only one there, so you had to do it. Someone had to. I told you that before."

"So maybe it was some stupid self-fulfilling prophecy. That doesn't excuse my behavior."

"Self-fulfilling? I didn't slap myself."

"But you planted the idea in my head. Honestly, all I could think about before I fell asleep was slapping you. I kept thinking how crazy it would be to slap my best friend."

I didn't know I was his best friend.

"Then it happened," he says. "And like I said, it's not your fault. I'm responsible for my actions. I'm really sorry."

For a second, I close my eyes and feel safe, like a child believing in a fairy tale. Then the growing pains hit me, rob me, and finish me off. I'm an adult again.

"Are you gonna accept my apology or what?" he says.

I look at the shriveled up hippo in the corner, with the wings that don't matter.

"Yeah," I say. "We're good."

#15

AT FIRST, I'M shocked to hear Cicely's voice in my home, and wonder how she found my number.

Then I remember that I'm listed several times in the phone book. I remember that I run two businesses. I remember that she once hired me, on the phone, to paint the outside of her house, and that's how we met in the first place.

"Nicholas?" she says, for maybe the 3rd time. "Cannibals get you?"

"Sorry," I say. "There was static."

I don't say, "In my head."

"Am I interrupting anything?" she says. "Ritual sacrifice? I could call back."

"No," I say. "I was working on a dental drill, but I need a break."

"I never would've pegged you as a dentist. Then again, I'm no good at guessing these things. As a child, I thought I'd grow up to be a penguin. Didn't pan out."

"I'm not a dentist." I can't help grinning. "I'm making a stuffed drill for some guy's retirement party. I make stuffed animals. Stuffed anything."

And I've crossed the line.

Cicely and me, we don't talk about work. Or anything, really.

We talk about man-eating vegetables and dancing linguini.

"That's perfect," she says, giggles.

I giggle back, on accident. I don't feel as stupid as I should.

"Look, hon," she says, and when Cicely says, "Look, hon," what she means is, "Look, hon."

"I'm calling because I have a problem," she says. "The earth-shattering, epic variety. Complete with state-of-the-art CGI battle sequences and a soundtrack by John Williams."

"That is a big problem."

"Part of me's saying, 'You can handle this, Cicely. You're a big girl now.' The other part of me's hiding under the bed, stuffing herself with comfort Twinkies."

"I can't help you," I say, too fast. "I mean, I want to help you, but I don't think I can. I'm not good at…helping." I want to stuff my mouth with polyfil, and sew up my lips once and for all.

"I don't expect you to solve my problem, if that's what you're afraid of."

"That's what I'm afraid of."

"I don't think anyone can solve my problem. Maybe if Jesus and Batman teamed up, but even then, they'd probably fail miserably."

I chortle with relief. I don't want to be Batman.

"What I want, is someone to talk to," she says. "I'd go to a therapist, but a therapist wouldn't believe me."

And she thinks I would.

And she's probably right.

"I wouldn't mind that," I say. "Listening to you."

"I'd like to talk about it in person, if that's OK. Over a couple steaming hot bowls of Thai curry?"

It must have slipped out once that this is my favorite food.

"We should eat something we'd both enjoy," I say.

I don't want her to sacrifice her Lists for mine.

More than Batman or Jesus, I don't want to be John.

"I like curry too," she says, soft. "Tonight at 6. Do you remember where my house is?"

"Yeah."

"See you then, hon."

"Bye."

I don't remember where her house is.

Lucky for me, I don't throw away any documents, and I find the address 20 minutes later in my closet. 2nd paper tower on the left.

The remaining 3 hours, I spend:

1. Biting my fingernails.
2. Contemplating whether or not I'm beyond biting my toenails.
3. Slapping myself in the face.
4. Knowing that no matter how hard or how many times I slap myself, it won't count as #15, the way playing solitaire doesn't count as a social life, and masturbating doesn't count as a sex life.
5. Hoping Cicely won't be #15.
6. Playing solitaire.
7. Masturbating.
8. Biting my toenails.

Then it's 6, and I'm inside Cicely's house, and my face burns more than a little.

I notice the tennis ball in her hand.

"Can I take your coat?" she says.

"Thanks," I say, and notice I'm not wearing one.

"Sorry. Stupid joke."

"It's not stupid."

She grins. "Well, make yourself comfortable, and I'll finish up the curry. Oh, and I wasn't sure what sort of meat you like. I ended up using Smurf. Hope that's OK."

"That's great."

She heads into the kitchen.

And I think she wants me to stay behind so that I can take a few moments to admire her work. And I do.

On one side of the room:

1. White walls.
2. A beige couch.
3. A cabinet filled with good china.
4. A grandfather clock.

And on the other side of the room:

1. An unfinished mural on the wall. I see Bigfoot riding a two-headed giraffe, jousting with an enormous baby on a motorcycle. And I see a

weeping cloud and a vampire on stilts trying to cheer him up with a finger-on-the-nose pig face.

2. A shelf topped with Godzilla figurines.

3. A lamp shaped like a monkey butler.

4. An army of garden gnomes lined up on the floor.

In other words, Cicely's personality is spreading throughout the room like a colorful virus.

No, like a smile spreading across my face.

"Food's ready!" Cicely says.

I find the kitchen/dining room area more like the boring half of the living room, except for the refrigerator door. There, I spot werewolves and other classic monsters, all flat and frozen in time.

On closer inspection, I notice a lone kitten in the middle of the magnetic mayhem. I point. "She's gotta be scared," I say.

"She's their leader," Cicely says. "They respect her because she's ruthless."

"Oh."

"Shall we eat?" she says.

We eat.

"This isn't Smurf," I say. "This is tofu with blue food coloring."

"I lied," she says. "I thought you might have a problem eating little people, being vegan and all."

"I appreciate the thought, but Smurfs aren't people. They're basically walking, talking plants. They use photosynthesis and everything."

"You learn something new everyday."

I laugh for maybe the 10th time since I walked in the front door.

Then I notice that Cicely's having trouble handling her fork. I notice that she's using her left hand, and that her right hand's under the table.

"This is good," I say. I don't just mean the food.

A door opens in the other room.

"Oh god," Cicely says, whispers.

I flinch when the tofu falls off my fork.

And a man steps into the kitchen. Compared to me, he's:

1. Taller.

2. More muscular.

3. Better looking.

He's the man I wanted to grow up to be.

"What are you doing here, John?" Cicely says.

"Who's this?" John says, pointing at my face.

"A friend."

For some reason, I stand and say, "We're eating curry."

John now aims his finger at Cicely. "Do you still have it?"

"Of course," she says.

"This is nuts, Cissy."

"That's your opinion."

He shakes his head, then sighs. "I know I said I wouldn't give you another chance. But…I love you. Let me have it, and we'll forget the whole thing."

"I can't do that, John."

"You can."

"I won't."

He glares at her, biting his lip.

Obviously, this is all my fault. I brought John here with my presence, and I deserve the guilt ravaging my innards.

John approaches Cicely.

She stands. She says, "Stay away from me."

But he doesn't. He grabs at the tennis ball, and she turns around to hold the ball away from him.

"Stop!" she says.

Instead of stopping, he pins her arms to her sides in a twisted embrace.

Cicely screams. There's panic in her voice that I'm sure has nothing to do with a tennis ball.

This is when I let go of my fork and charge. I punch John as hard as I can on the side of his chest.

He doesn't fall over crying like I hope, but he does let go of Cicely.

I've never experienced a fight in real life. So I expect a fair amount of talking.

Some quips and comebacks, maybe. I don't expect to be punched in the face so soon. I don't expect the silence as John knocks me onto the floor, and slaps me 5 times.

He'd keep slapping me, I'm sure, but Cicely kicks his spine.

"I'm sorry," she says. She's crying.

John gets off me, rubbing his face with both hands. "This is stupid," he says. And he walks away.

Cicely kneels beside me, ball in hand. "Are you OK?" she says.

"Yeah," I say, crackle. "I'm fine."

"Thank you."

"It was nothing."

"No," she says, and a smile spreads across her face. "You just saved the world."

Cicely:

> 1. Deadbolts the front door.
>
> 2. Applies olive oil to my face. She says, "This'll help."
>
> 3. Tells me her earth-shattering, epic problem.

And I:

> 1. Laugh.
>
> 2. Apologize for laughing.
>
> 3. Almost believe her.

"I woke up and I felt the ball in my hand and I knew," Cicely says. "I don't know how else to explain it. I also don't know how to say it without sounding like a crazy person."

"You don't sound crazy," I say.

"You're sweet." She squeezes my arm.

"I'm not sweet," I almost say. Instead, I touch my throbbing face with my throbbing fingers.

"For over a week, I couldn't get myself to leave the house," she says. "The responsibility paralyzed me."

"That makes sense."

"I'm still terrified something's going to happen, but I'm not going to stop living my life."

"I'm glad."

She smiles. "You don't believe any of this, do you?"

"I believe you." I hope I don't sound sarcastic.

"It's OK to tell me the truth, hon," she says. "I'm still doubting myself 100 times a day. I can't tell you how many times I've almost let go of the ball. But any time I get close, the truth hits me again, and I've never been so certain about anything in my life."

"I get slapped every day."

She laughs. Then apologizes for laughing.

"I can't stop it from happening," I say.

"When did this start?" she says.

"About 2 weeks ago."

"God," she says, whispers. "Mine too."

#16

IN MY DREAM, Cicely's my sister. I'm trying to tell her how sorry I am that I lost her ball, and killed everyone, but she can't hear me. Or maybe she's ignoring me.

I notice a man outside the window. He's watching us. He's ugly, with hair crawling out his ears, but he's still John.

Then my sister's body contorts. Her elbows bend the wrong way and her torso caves in and she blinks so fast.

I can't scream.

Outside of this nightmare, awake, I escape to Sol's house. In this house, there's:

    1. No alcohol.

    2. No swearing.

    3. No surprises.

"You don't have to keep buying these," I say, and hand him his winged hippo.

"You think I buy them out of charity?" he says.

"Sol, you hate animals."

"I don't hate animals. I don't like pets in the house is all."

"You're honestly trying to tell me that if I wasn't your son, you'd still have a zoo of flying creatures on that shelf?"

"OK, OK. Maybe it did start out as charity. But they grew on me." He pets the hippo. "Before now, I've never been one for collections."

"Because they cost money."

"No, I could collect shells. That doesn't cost anything."

"You'd have to pay for gas to go to the beach."

"OK." He grins. "The point is, I'm glad I finally have something to collect.

Anytime someone comes over, they ask me about the animals. I get to tell them my son made them. They're always very impressed."

I know that's not true.

And this is a conversation we've had maybe 10 times before.

It doesn't matter.

Sol places the winged hippo next to the winged anteater, which he always calls a bear. I don't correct him.

"There," Sol says, and claps his hands.

The sound makes me jump.

I notice that my hand's touching my face, so I pretend to scratch an itch.

"I'd better head back," I say.

I don't want to, really. I want to move back into my old room, where all the exercise equipment is now, and I want to sleep there every night, forever.

But I can't.

The longer I stay here, the more likely Sol will be #16.

"I have a girlfriend," Sol says. He's hugging himself tight, a shield over his heart.

"Oh," I say.

I didn't think there'd be another surprise in this house after my mother disappeared. I didn't think Sol would ever stop waiting. He told me he'd never stop waiting.

"Congratulations," I say. And part of me means it, maybe.

He smiles.

I try.

"Her name's Brienda," he says. "She likes your animals too."

I can't scream. Instead, I say, I manage, "I'm glad."

Cicely believes someone did this to us.

She thinks that this someone snuck into our rooms in the dead of night, and put the tennis ball in her hand, and, I don't know, kissed my cheek wearing unholy ChapStick.

But I know the truth.

I know that I brought this on myself.

And as for Cicely's earth-shattering, epic problem, the Universe or God decided it's sick and tired of making the big decisions. Now it's time for a human being to choose the fate of the world. And not just any human being. The best humanity has to offer.

But I don't tell Cicely any of this.

I'm too embarrassed.

Cicely reaches over and taps my cheek with her left palm. "Do you think that counts?" she says.

"I don't know," I say.

"If it does, I'll give you a baby slap every morning."

"Thank you." And my face may be on fire.

"By the way, I called Nancy Drew earlier, but she won't take our case," Cicely says. "And the Hardy Boys quit sleuthing two years ago to start a cake decorating business in San Luis Obispo. It looks like we're on our own."

I chuckle.

Cicely studies the tennis ball, close, as if searching for clues. And maybe she'll find one. "We need to figure out who and what we have in common," she says. "Maybe we were targeted for a reason."

So Cicely and me, instead of just talking about man-eating vegetables and dancing linguini, we cross more lines. And I write it all down in a little purple notebook.

We compare:

1. Enemies. My List here, of course, is very long. And to my surprise, so is Cicely's. "Oh, and I almost forgot," Cicely says. "There's also Gargamel. I know what you're thinking. I eat Smurfs for breakfast, so he and I should be the best of friends. But there was this whole re-gifting incident that got blown way out of proportion. It's a long story."

2. Friends. And my List here, of course, isn't very long. Then Cicely says, "Hey, don't forget about me." And I smile and I say, "And Cicely."

3. Family. "They're all on my Enemies List," Cicely says. She doesn't tell me any more about that, and I don't pry.

4. Places we've lived. "I don't care how cheap the waterfront property is," Cicely says. "Take my advice: stay out of the Bizarro World. Their healthcare system's even shoddier than it is here, if you can believe it. Worst 3 years of my life."

5. Places we've worked. And I'm sure Cicely's joking about the DMV, but it turns out she isn't.

6. Schools. "I knew I should have gone to Hogwarts," Cicely says.

And we end up comparing:

7. Favorite books.

8. Favorite movies.

9. Favorite songs.

10. Favorite foods.

11. Favorite colors.

On and on, until it's dark outside.

"OK," Cicely says, and examines the commonalities I circled in my little purple notebook. "All we have to do now is find someone who hates organic foods, the color green, and the films of Terry Gilliam. Then whammo, mystery solved."

On the way home, I get into a fender-bender with a Cadillac. It's my fault, like usual, and the driver of the other car doesn't cope with the situation very well.

In other words, Cicely's baby slap didn't count.

#17

THIS ISN'T THE first time I've found Gordon crying and sniffling on the couch, petting Meta with both hands. And I'm sure it's not the last.

"Nick?" he says. "Can we talk?"

"Yeah," I say.

Gordon doesn't wipe the tears off his face. "Things have gotten awkward between us since I punched you."

He didn't punch me, but I don't correct him this time.

"Yeah," I say, whisper. "I'm sorry."

He laughs out his nose, which causes some snot to spurt out. This he does wipe away. "I'm sorry for laughing. You just sounded so doom and gloomy. I should've told you I was listening to *Six Feet Under* a minute ago. Hence the tears."

"Oh."

"Anyway, I wanted to bring the awkwardness out in the open, because I find talking about it makes the awkwardness less awkward. Does that make sense?"

"I think so."

We sit in silence for a while.

"Great plan," I say.

He laughs, and the silence that follows is more comfortable.

"Remember when we used to talk philosophy?" Gordon says.

"Yeah," I say. When he first moved in, that's about all we did.

"Jesus fuck, that was fun. Why did we stop?"

"I don't know. Maybe we figured everything out."

He laughs again. "I guess so."

And in a way, that's true. Six months ago we agreed on the meaning of life.

We agreed that the meaning of life is to get so wrapped up in living that you don't care about the meaning anymore.

I stare at the half-finished Elvis on the floor.

He's:

> 1. Naked.

> 2. Empty.

> 3. Alone.

"What do you know about missing people?" I say.

"Is this a philosophical question?" Gordon says.

"No, I mean, statistics."

"It depends on what country you're talking about. Is there a genocide going on?"

"In the US."

"Ah," he says, in a gentle way, like he realizes I'm talking about my mom. Maybe he does. "About 10% of missing people never go home again, but that doesn't mean they're dead. Sometimes they start over somewhere else."

I think about my mom kissing another husband and telling another son that she loves him more than the world itself. I'd hate her for this, obviously. But this is a much better nightmare than the ones where she's decomposing in the ground or chained up in a basement with rats that chew her in her sleep.

"You know what really pisses me off?" Gordon says. "Missing kids."

"Yeah, they're real bastards."

"Shut up, Nick. It's not the kids. It's the whole down-with-strangers campaign. As if they're the problem. But you know what, Nick? It's not strangers who kidnap kids. It's not strangers who fuck them up. It hardly ever happens that way."

"I get what you're saying," I say. "But why does that piss you off?"

"I don't know. Maybe the world would be a better place if people focused more on real problems instead of so many imaginary ones."

But maybe it's not always so easy to tell the difference. I don't tell Gordon that. Instead, I say, "Yeah."

Cicely invites me over again. I know:

    1. Going to Cicely's house could make her #17.

    2. My presence attracts acts of aggression, so I'd be putting Cicely in danger.

    3. I'd be putting the whole world in danger.

I go to Cicely's house.

"Did it work?" she says.

At first I don't know what she's talking about. Then I remember, and shake my head. "Thanks for trying though."

"I'm sorry."

"It's alright. It's really not so bad."

She takes my hand. "Bad or not so bad, you don't deserve this."

"Yes I do," I almost say. Instead, I look down at my hand in Cicely's hand, and she's covering up all the scars on my knuckles.

She looks me in the eyes, and says, "We'll figure it out."

"Yeah," I say. I almost believe her.

She only releases my hand when the phone rings.

"Hello," she says into the plastic banana phone. And she's silent for a while. "If you're going to make a prank call, at least come up with something original, you...booger fork." She hangs up.

"What was that about?" I say.

"I'll show you." She walks into her bedroom, and I think she wants me to follow her, so I get up from the couch.

But she comes back with a piece of paper. She gives it to me.

On the paper, it says "CURSED?" in bold letters, with Cicely's phone number underneath.

"I've been posting them around town," she says. "In case we're not the only ones."

"Oh," I say, and I want us to be the only ones. I want to rip up the paper like a child.

I feel stupid.

"So far I've only received prank calls," she says. "Including the young gentleman who was just explaining what a terrible curse it is to have such an enormous, um, membrum virile."

"I see."

"But maybe there's someone out there with a real problem, like singing eyelashes or evil hemorrhoids."

"Aren't all hemorrhoids evil?"

"Yes, but these are really evil. They steal candy from babies, then make the babies watch them eat it."

I don't have to ask Cicely why she's searching for other people like us.

Another person:

    1. Might mean more clues.

But even more important than that:

    2. Might need someone to talk to.

Cicely and me, we don't solve The Mystery of the Curses. Instead we:

    1. Discuss the film, *Brazil*. "I don't care what anyone says," Cicely says. "The real heroes are the ducts."

    2. Watch the film, *Attack of the Giant Leeches*. "Real giant leeches don't kill like that," Cicely says.

    3. Eat soup. "I'll bring the food tomorrow," I say, afterward.

But Cicely didn't suggest a meeting tomorrow. And I stare into my empty bowl.

"Sounds good," Cicely says.

"What should I bring?" I say.

"Anything but leech. After the movie, I don't think I have the stomach for them anymore."

I check my watch.

The time's 10:44.

"I'd better go," I say. "If I don't, John might show up again."

I don't say, "Or you might slap me."

I don't say, "I'm afraid."

In fact, there's a lot I don't say.

What I manage is, "Thanks for the soup."

I'm waiting outside the apartment with Elvis. My plan was to work on him to keep my mind off the inevitable. But he's still:

1. Naked.

2. Empty.

3. Alone.

Even in my company, he looks alone.

The time's 11:27.

And I'm outside because Gordon's inside. I locked myself out. I hope that's enough.

#17, or who I assume is #17, turns out to be Karl.

He tells me the same old story.

The story that my ex-girlfriend told me 11 days ago, before she slapped me.

The story that my ex-teacher told me 15 days ago, before he slapped me.

The story about how he dropped his phone book, and it landed open on the floor, and he spotted my name, as if the words were hovering on the page. Or about how he happened to overhear a co-worker talking about me and the stuffed toaster I crafted for her.

"Seriously," Karl says. "I'm not shitting you."

And I act surprised.

"It's funny us both ending up here after all these years," he says.

"Funny," I say.

"Is it just me, or didn't you swear you'd never set foot in this muck bucket again?"

"Muck bucket?"

"I mean the town, man. You always called it that."

"That doesn't sound like me. I'd call it a shithole, sure. Craptown, maybe. Never muck bucket."

"You're still an asshole, I see."

"Nah, I'm recovering. That was a momentary relapse."

"So why'd you move back?"

"It just felt like the right thing to do."

"Same here. What's that on your leg?"

"A doll."

"What're you doing with a doll on your leg?"

"I don't know."

"So. You wanna celebrate our little reunion with a couple drinks? Tomorrow night?"

"I thought…." And I decide not to finish my sentence.

"Yeah, I was dry for a while. Didn't take. Me and Heather separated, and I moved back here. And I've got to do something with my free time, right? But I've cut way back, man. Things are a lot better now." And he goes on to explain why he doesn't need any help, and why he's different from every other alcoholic who's ever lived. In other words, he's talking to me the way I used to talk to myself.

"Uh huh," I say.

And maybe Karl started drinking again because he couldn't cope with Heather learning about his infidelity and leaving him, and I know how easy it is to relapse. I know the statistics, because Gordon's told me.

But maybe Karl started drinking again so that he could be here tonight, sitting with me on my doorstep, and maybe it's all my fault.

"So what do you say?" Karl says.

"I can't," I say.

"Fuck, man. Don't tell me you've dried up."

"Yeah."

"I mean, good for you, man. You were out of control. But this sucks."

"I'm sorry."

"Shit. We could celebrate without the drinks. Fuck the drinks."

"I'm actually…really busy." The truth is, I'm afraid to be around him. "I'm sorry."

"Fuck you, Nick."

And this is the same old story about a person's past, and how there's nowhere left to hide.

I squeeze Elvis tight.

#18

CICELY INFORMS ME that she's busy taming a wild Chupacabra and asks if I'll please leave a message after the beep.

Then I say, "Hi Cicely. This is Nicholas, AKA the idiot who said he'd make you dinner, completely forgetting that today's his step-dad's birthday party. I can probably come over by 8, if that's alright with you. I…hope it is. I'll talk to you later. Bye."

I call back and say, "I'm really losing it, Cicely. I forgot to apologize. I'm sorry. That sorry was for forgetting to apologize, and this one's for the dinner fiasco: I'm sorry. I…um…bye."

And I want to destroy my messages with the power of my mind.

I also want to call her again and invite her to the party, because I don't want to face my sister or Sol's new girlfriend alone. And with Cicely in the room or the grocery store or wherever we are, I don't feel alone.

But I don't call her again.

She has enough problems to deal with. Plus the dinner starts in 15 minutes.

10 minutes later, I'm hugging Sol, a little tighter than usual.

He says, "My son. My son." This is what he always says when he hugs me, and it always makes me feel a little sad. I don't know why.

It doesn't matter.

"Happy birthday, Dad," I say.

"I hope you're hungry," he says. "Brienda made us quite a feast."

"That's good."

"Let's join the table before they start without us, hm?"

"Yeah."

I don't want to, really. I want to stay here, hugging Sol, feeling loved and a little sad, until everyone else goes away.

But I can't.

Sol and me, we join the others.

I give out hugs around the table.

1. "I'm so glad to see you," Nadia says, and when Nadia says, "so," what she means is, "not."
2. Svetlana shows me the doll that I made for her 1st birthday. It's her favorite, and I don't think her parents are very happy about that.
3. Greg doesn't say anything.
4. "It's wonderful to finally meet you," Brienda says.

"Yeah," I say.

"I told Brienda that you're a vagan," Sol says.

Nadia corrects him.

"Vegan," he says. "So she made us a lot of vegan dishes."

"That's great," I say. I didn't mean to sound so quiet. So unimpressed.

"Have you talked to your doctor about your diet?" Nadia says. "I've read a lot of horror stories about what veganism can do to your body."

"I'm fine," I say.

She places her hand on mine. "I just don't want you to get sick."

"I know."

"Let's eat," Sol says.

We eat.

After the cake, Sol opens his presents at the table.

"How cute!" Brienda says.

"Just what I wanted," Sol says, and pats the penguin's head. "Thank you, Nicholas."

"I want to hold it," Svetlana says.

"What do we say, Svetlana?" Nadia says.

"Please, Grandpa?"

"Be careful with it," Sol says, handing it to her. "It's very precious."

Svetlana carries it around the room on top of her open palms, as if it is very precious.

"Why does it have an extra pair of wings?" Greg says.

"I collect flying animals," Sol says.

"But penguins can already fly."

"I don't think they can," I say.

"I'm sure I've seen them flying on documentaries we've watched," Greg says. "I can clearly picture it in my mind."

"I think he's right," Nadia says. And of course she's referring to Greg.

"Well, they're magical wings then," I say. "They let him travel to other dimensions."

Greg smiles and leans back in his chair with his arms crossed.

"Grandpa!" Svetlana says, and runs to his side. "I dropped it!"

"It's OK," Sol says. "You can pick it up again. It's OK."

"OK." She runs off again.

"Walk," Nadia and Greg say together.

"I think it's a wonderful gift, Nicholas," Brienda says. "You're a very skilled young man."

"Thank you," I say.

She smiles.

I try.

"You're a good cook," I say.

"Thank you!" she says. "I'll cook for you whenever you like. Just say the word."

And Brienda, she's:

1. Too short.
2. Too heavy.
3. Too loud.
4. Too friendly.
5. Too happy.

In other words, she's not my mother.

And I hate her for that.

I hate her so much in this moment that maybe it shows all over my face.

Sol slaps me hard. But it's not really me he's attacking. He's fighting his own guilt and grief, and that's what I tell myself as I hold back my tears with the power of my mind.

"Oh," Sol says. He looks at me with those I-don't-know-what-got-into-me eyes. And I want to tell him exactly what it is.

But he wouldn't believe me.

No one here would believe me, except Svetlana.

"Sol," Brienda says, hard, and maybe she'll never forgive him.

"I'm sorry," Sol says, soft, and maybe he'll never forgive himself.

And I don't put a hand on Sol's shoulder.

Instead, I say, "You told me you'd wait for Mom. You promised me. But here you are, messing around with another woman, and you expect me to be OK with it?" The words come out fast and easy. "Fuck you, Sol."

"Nicholas," Sol says.

"I think you'd better leave," Nadia says.

"Fuck you too," I say.

I leave the house, alone, and now they'll be able to forgive themselves, and each other.

And I know:

    1. I dropped something very precious inside me.

    2. It feels broken.

On my answering machine, Cicely tells me not to worry about the dinner. She also asks me to bring over some tiny stakes, if I have any, as her house is infested by a pack of vampiric cockroaches.

When I approach her front door, I notice that her welcome mat no longer says "WELCOME" in bold letters, with a few flowers underneath. Now it looks like a pirate flag and it says "AHOY!" And there's a wind chime above me, made out of hanging sporks.

Cicely lets me inside with a smile.

"Here," I say, and hand her the box of toothpicks that I bought on the way here.

She stares at the box, as if trying to decipher the meaning, and then she does. She laughs. "Those roaches may have won the battle, but now I'll win the war."

I can't help glancing at the tennis ball, because it's duct taped to the back of her hand.

"I tape it when I'm painting," she says.

"Ah," I say, and I study the mural on the wall. I see a dragon in a top hat, tap dancing on the stomach of a sleeping Matador. And I see an alien vomiting out his UFO with the upchuck heading towards a sweaty angel on a unicycle.

Then I sit beside Cicely, and watch her unravel the duct tape. Afterward, she rolls the ball from the back of her hand to her palm, careful and slow. She holds on tight.

I can breathe again.

"Why don't you tape it all the time?" I say. I could probably figure this out myself if I thought about it hard enough, but I don't want to.

"Well," she says. "I'm afraid if I kept it taped for too long, I'd forget that it's there, and I'd make some stupid mistake. And then, poof."

"Is that what the end of the world sounds like?"

"Either that or kablam."

"I always thought it was kablammo."

"No, that's the sound of a spleen spontaneously combusting."

"What about kazooey?"

"Hm. That's the sound of a robot's mechanical heart when it falls in love."

"You're very knowledgeable."

And maybe I'm not laughing as much as usual.

Because after a while, Cicely says, "Is everything OK?"

I want to tell her the truth, but I don't want to add to her list of worries. I know she already has:

1. John.

Not to mention:

2. The entire world.

When Cicely takes my hand, a few tears escape me. And a few more.

"It's the whole slapping thing," I say, crackle. "I'm really starting to lose it."

"I'm so sorry," she says.

I'm not Gordon, so I wipe away more and more tears.

Cicely puts her arm around me.

And the power of my mind isn't strong enough anymore.

The pain floods out, fast and easy.

Cicely:

    1. Holds me tighter.

    2. Says, "We'll get through this together, hon."

    3. Doesn't let me go.

If I wasn't crying so hard, I might smile.

#19

IN MY DREAM, Karl's my roommate again. I'm trying to tell him how sorry I am that Heather died when I crashed the car, but he can't hear me. Or maybe he's ignoring me.

I notice a man outside the window. He's watching us. He's ugly, with bones poking out his face, but he's still Sol.

Then my roommate's body contorts. His flesh folds over and over, until he's a rag doll on the floor.

I can't help him.

Outside of this nightmare, awake, I escape to the kitchen.

"Morning," Gordon says. He's:

1. Sitting on his stool.
2. Crunching on granola.
3. Petting Meta with his bare feet.

"I need help," I say.

"What with?"

"I need you to slap me."

"Jesus fuck, Nick."

"You'd be doing me a favor. Seriously."

He puts down his spoon. "How's that exactly?"

"If you don't slap me, someone else will. I'd rather it be you."

He snorts. "That's almost flattering, in a twisted sort of way, but I'm not gonna slap you."

"Consider it an experiment in the psychology of violence."

"I'm not a scientist."

"Please." And I sound as desperate as I feel, maybe. "I really need your help with this."

He sighs. "Slapping you isn't gonna help, Nick. You've subconsciously constructed this sort of masochistic road to redemption, and I'm not gonna be one of your potholes. I'm not an enabler, remember? That's why you wanted me as your roommate in the first place."

"This isn't something I'm doing to myself, Gordon. This is affecting everyone around me."

"Of course it is! We're all fucking connected. Anyway, I don't want to hurt you anymore. I'm not a violent person, and punching you the other night was semi-traumatic for me. I'm still trying to get over it."

"I'm sorry."

"Thanks." He picks up his spoon again.

"I've been slapped 18 days in a row."

"That's weird," he says, and goes back to petting Meta with his bare feet and crunching his granola.

In other words, Gordon can't help me.

I see Santa trapped in a mason jar, boxing with a furry octopus. And I see a painted-on crack in the wall with swirling darkness on the other side and 2 slivers of eye peeking through.

"He's the one who did this to us," Cicely says, and points at the slivers with her tennis ball. "This booger fork thinks he can hide from us, but I'll find him. They don't call me X-Ray Eyes for nothing."

I take my spot on the couch.

Cicely, hers.

"Maybe I'm just paranoid about John coming back," she says. "But lately I've felt like someone's watching me."

"Me too," I say.

But even before I brought the curse on myself, I felt the eyes on me. They're the eyes of the Universe or God, and they don't watch me because I'm playing some big part in the fate of the world or because I'm the best humanity has to offer.

I don't tell Cicely any of this.

Instead, I say, "I need help."

She takes my hand. "What can I do, hon?"

And I want her to be more than my friend right now. I want her to be the hand of fate, slapping me across the face, saving me from my road to redemption.

And I know:

1. Cicely would slap me if I asked.

2. She'd feel terrible about it afterward.

3. She'd do it again tomorrow.

"I was bit by one of those vampire roaches," I say. "And I don't know how this works exactly. Am I gonna turn into a vampire or a bug or both?"

"Well, there's good news and bad news," she says. "What do you want first?"

"Good." Because good should always come first.

"When it comes to vampiric insect attacks, there usually aren't any transmogrifying effects."

"That's a relief. What's the bad news?"

"Evil hemorrhoids."

"I should've known."

Cicely and me, we don't solve The Mystery of the Curses.

Instead, we sit in silence for a while, and Cicely doesn't let go of my hand, even when the phone rings.

"Do you want to take this one?" she says.

"What do you mean?" I say.

"The fairy that lives in my ear is getting a little tired of the prank calls. I promised her I'd take a break for a while. Do you mind?"

"No," I say. I scramble for the plastic banana. "Hello? This is Cicely. I mean, Cicely's house. Can I help you?"

I want to hide under the pastel labyrinth of a rug.

"Hi Cicely," a man says. "I lost my wife last Tuesday." He laughs. "That sounds like she died. I should say the divorce was finalized last Tuesday. I didn't think it would hit me this hard, because I've been divorced three times before. But this one, it's worse than all the others combined. I feel like such a failure, but I have no idea what I did wrong this time. I was a good husband to her. I feel so doomed."

And I have a feeling he thinks this is some kind of hotline.

I suppose it is.

"We don't really handle that sort of problem," I say.

"Oh," he says.

"But, um, I'm sure you'll find the right person eventually."

He laughs. "How could you possibly know that? Most people don't ever find the right person, do they?"

"I don't know. But if you do find her, and things work out, you'll be thanking God for all these divorces, right?"

"I don't believe in God, but I guess you're right." He sighs, and releases something doom and gloomy in that breath, maybe. "Thanks, Cicely."

"No problem."

He hangs up.

I sit down.

"That was real, wasn't it?" Cicely says.

"Either that or the most obscure prank call of all time," I say. "But it wasn't our kind of curse."

"No singing eyelashes, huh?"

"Not a one."

"You did a good job, hon. I think you helped him."

And there are many eyes on me when I say, "Thanks." The eyes of:

    1. God or the Universe.

    2. The creature in the swirling darkness.

    3. John, maybe, hiding outside.

But the only eyes I can really feel right now belong to:

    4. Cicely.

Greg opens the door, but leaves the screen door closed. "If you're here to apologize, Nadia's not here," he says.

"I'm not here to apologize," I say.

"What then?"

"I drove all the way out here to talk to you. Thirty minutes. The least you can do is let me inside."

The least he can do is slam the door in my face.

But he opens the screen and says, "Alright." I'm sure he didn't mean to sound so eager. So thrilled.

"Thank you," I say. I step through the threshold, arms crossed.

"Sit down," he says.

I do.

He doesn't.

He looks down at me, smiling, and says, "What is it you want to talk about?"

"I want to show you something," I say. I unfold the printout I've been squeezing, and hand it to Greg.

He's more than my brother-in-law right now, even if he doesn't know it. He's my chance to take control.

"What is this?" he says.

"I found it on a website," I say. "A website for elementary school kids."

He scans the page some more. I thought about highlighting the vital sentence beforehand, but this is better.

Then his smile drops. His eyes narrow.

"You're lucky Nadia doesn't care about the size of a man's brain," I say.

I wonder if I sound as childish as I feel.

I hope so.

Greg:

    1. Slaps me. And maybe it is really me he's attacking.

    2. Points to the door.

    3. Says, "Go home."

I can't think of anything else to say but, "Thank you."

Then I pick up my printout about penguins and obey.

#20

RIGHT NOW THEY'RE a happy couple on the beach, holding hands, maybe experiencing a moment of pure joy.

But when I get through with them, they'll be:

1. A psychopathic bride, stained with blood.

2. A severed head, dripping that blood.

I put the photograph of the couple into my pocket, where it joins the company of:

1. The crumpled up penguin printout.

Though I already know penguins can't fly.

2. The paper from my closet, 2nd stack on the left.

Though I've already memorized Cicely's address.

3. This week's to-do list

4. This week's to-make list.

Though there isn't much on either of those.

5. My little purple notebook.

Though I remember everything Cicely told me about herself.

So maybe I don't need all this.

It doesn't matter.

Every few hours today, I'm going to:

1. Sit down.

2. Empty my pockets.

3. Examine the bits and pieces of my life.

Because if I don't, I might make too many stupid mistakes. And then, poof. That's the sound of the world I've created for myself crumbling away.

I check my watch.

The time's 9:14.

2 hours and 46 minutes more, then I'll go to Cicely's for lunch.

I get back to work.

I'm in the middle of hand-stitching the body form of my octopus closed when someone knocks on the door.

My heart thuds hard.

I know that everyone in my family uses this knock, but I can't help trembling as I reach for the knob.

It's my mother's knock too.

I open the door.

"Sol," I say.

He hugs me, a little softer than usual. He says, "My son. My son."

It makes me feel more than a little sad, and this time I know why.

"You didn't have to drive all the way here," I say. "You could've called me. I would've come over."

"Let's sit down for a while, hm?" he says.

I nod.

We sit inside.

"I'm sorry I didn't call," I say. "I didn't know how to apologize for what I said. I thought I'd try making you an apology octopus."

"What's an apology octopus?" Sol says.

I point to the winged octopus sitting in the corner.

"I'm not sure what good the wings would do for him," I say. "Since he can't breathe out of water."

"Maybe he's good at holding his breath," Sol says.

"I'm sorry I said what I said before. I didn't mean it."

"You did, Nicholas."

"No." Suddenly, I feel like a child again.

"You shouldn't have yelled at me. You shouldn't have cursed at me or your sister. I'll accept your apology for these things you did, but I'm glad you told me the truth."

"It wasn't the truth. Really."

"You're going to have to apologize for lying now, if you keep this up."

"Sorry."

"I'm sorry too. I should never have slapped you."

"It wasn't your fault."

"It was, Nicholas. I want you to know why I did it."

"I know why."

He rubs his knees with his hands. "Ever since Brienda and I became friends, I tried not to think about your mother at all. That's a terrible thing, I know. I knew all the time how terrible it was, but I didn't care. Then I saw you glaring at Brienda at the party, hating her, I thought, for being a part of my life. And in that moment, I hated her too, and I hated myself for loving her. I blamed you for that. That's why I slapped you. But all that hatred was already inside me. Please forgive me."

I want to:

1. Tell him the slap wasn't his fault.

2. Tell him all his hatred came from my curse, and that there's only love in his heart.

3. Keep believing in this fairy tale, forever.

Instead, I say, "Alright. I forgive you."

He slaps his knees and stands, grinning.

We hug again, at the door.

"I don't hate her," I say. "Brienda."

"I'm glad," Sol says.

We say goodbye.

I don't want to, really. I want to tell Sol not to love Brienda too much, because mom could be back any day now, and not to do the family knock in front of Brienda, ever.

But I can't.

Instead, I close the door.

My watch beeps at 11:15, and it's time for #2 on my to-do list.

I'm not looking forward to this one.

Before dialing the number, I study my list, close, as if searching for clues. But I don't find any.

I make the call.

"This is Greg," Greg says.

"This is Nicholas," I say, and I feel stupid already. "I'm sorry about yesterday."

"Right."

"I really am, Greg."

"OK."

"Can I speak to Nadia, please?"

"She's busy."

"I want to apologize. Can you tell her I'm on the phone?"

He sighs static. "Alright."

I wait, with my to-do list on my knee, and the paper covers up my large starburst of scar. I used to tell people the wound came from a:

1. Fight with someone I didn't even know.
2. Fall from the 7th floor of a hotel.
3. Mountain lion attack.

I never mentioned:

1. The treadmill.

Or:

2. The crying.

Or:

3. The puppy Sol and my mom bought me for being so brave, even though I wasn't at all.

"Hello?" Nadia says.

"It's me," I say. "I'm calling because I'm sorry. For what I said." The words come out slow and awkward, though I should be an expert in contrition by now. "I'm really sorry, Nadia."

"It's not me you should be apologizing to," she says. "You should apologize to Svetlana for scaring her."

"Alright. Put her on the phone."

There's a pause, then she says, "I don't want you talking to her right now."

I sigh. "I see."

"Have you started drinking again, Nicky?" and when Nadia says, "Nicky," what she means is, "my stupid baby brother."

"No," I say.

"You sounded drunk at the party."

"I wasn't."

"Greg thinks so too."

"Well, then, it must be true."

"I just don't want to lose you again, Nicky."

"I know. I'm fine. Really."

"I wish I could believe that."

My watch beeps.

"I'd better go," I say.

"I'll tell Svetlana that you're sorry," she says.

"Thanks." And I really mean that. "Maybe I could make her another doll."

"She has enough dolls."

"OK, well, I'll talk to you later."

"Goodbye, Nicky."

I draw a big X over:

2. Nadia.

And I press a little too hard, so the pen pokes through the paper. Now there's a little black dot in my middle of my starburst. I lick my finger to wash the mistake away.

But I change my mind.

Instead, I add:

1. Another dot.

2. A curved line.

Now there's a little happy face on my knee.

It doesn't make me:

1. Smile.

2. Laugh.

3. Feel any better.

But Cicely might like it.

That's enough.

I see an unfinished jackalope balancing on the colossal nose of an albino Viking, but that's only because it's difficult for me to look at Cicely's face as she's saying, "He's a monster. A real monster."

And I'm sure:

1. Somehow, she means me.

2. She hates me.

3. She's going to slap me, hard.

I want to close my eyes.

"Abby will be out of the bathroom soon," Cicely says. "She'll tell you the whole story."

"Who's Abby?" I say.

"I'm sorry. I'm not making much sense, am I? I'm so upset."

But upset isn't the word I'd use.

The fury in her forehead reminds me of John, and the grim passion in her eyes reminds me of Sol, when he held my shoulders years ago, squeezing so hard it hurt, and he said, "They'll find her, Nicholas."

"Abby's one of us," Cicely says. "She saw one of my flyers and called."

Then Abby returns from the bathroom.

Compared to Cicely, she's:

1. Younger, by 25 years, maybe.

2. Smaller.

And some might say she's:

3. Better looking.

She's the woman I wanted to grow up to marry, except:

1. Her eyebrows are a little bushy.

2. She's missing her left thumb.

3. She's a real person, with real problems, and I never really wanted that.

"Is this him?" Abby says.

"It's him," Cicely says.

Abby approaches me and holds out her hand.

I take it. She's either very cold, or I'm very hot.

It doesn't matter.

"I'm Abby," she says. "It's not short for Abigail or anything. It's my real name."

"Oh," I say. "I'm Nicholas. It's not short for anything either."

"What would Nicholas be short for?"

"Never mind."

"Shall we sit?" Cicely says.

We sit.

And Abby takes my usual spot next to Cicely.

I want this girl gone already.

"Could you tell him what you told me?" Cicely says.

Abby nods.

"Are you ready?" Cicely says, to me.

I can't think of anything else to say but, "Yeah."

Abby picks at a scab on her arm. She doesn't look at me when she says, "I woke up one morning, and my family was gone."

"I'm sorry," I say.

"I tore up the house looking for any sign of them, but I couldn't find anything. Not anything."

Cicely holds her close.

"Isn't this a case for the police?" I say, fast and easy, because I'm:

    1. Jealous.

    2. Stupid.

"They wouldn't believe me," Abby says.

"Show him the photograph," Cicely says.

Abby pulls a photo out of her jeans pocket, and hands it over.

There's Abby, standing in a luscious garden, nowhere close to a moment of pure joy, judging by her face.

"They're all like that," Abby says, and tugs at her scab with two fingers. "I'm always alone, you know? And I called everyone I know, and they don't remember anything about my family at all. They said I live alone in that house. And there's no records of my family anywhere or anything."

"Oh," I say, handing the photo back.

"The worst part is, I don't remember anything about my family either. I know they're missing, because they're like holes inside me, you know? I have a mom and a dad and a brother, and we were all living together, and that's all the family I have, but I don't know anything else. I don't know what to do. I don't know why this happened to me."

Her cut's bleeding now.

And Cicely looks like she did when I first came in. I imagine her squeezing the tennis ball so hard, it pops.

"Guess when this all started," Cicely says.

"19 days ago," I say.

Abby nods.

Cicely whispers in her ear.

I'm sitting on the chair to the side of the couch, and I can see the creature in the swirling darkness, staring at Abby and Cicely from behind.

And maybe someone did:

1. Sneak into our rooms in the dead of night.
2. Put a tennis ball in Cicely's hand.
3. Kiss my cheek wearing unholy ChapStick.
4. Zap Abby's family out of her life. Or out of existence altogether.

Maybe this has:

1. Nothing to do with the Universe or God or my road to redemption.
2. Everything to do with a sick bastard who gets off on fucking with people's lives.

But I don't tell Cicely or Abby any of this.

"You're bleeding," Cicely says, touching Abby's arm. "I'll get you a Band-Aid." She heads for the bathroom.

I look at Abby.

I don't say, "What happened to your thumb?"

I don't say, "I wish you would leave."

What I do say is, "I'm sorry about your family."

"Thanks," Abby says, staring at the happy face on my knee.

It doesn't make her:

    1. Smile.

    2. Laugh.

    3. Feel any better, I'm sure.

So I lick my finger, and wash the smile away.

Cicely's her old smiling self when she places a heart-shaped plate on the middle of the table.

"I hope you all like komodo dragon sandwiches," she says.

And the world's right in the kitchen again.

Abby stares at the sandwiches with wide eyes.

"I'm kidding, hon," Cicely says.

I want to tell her not to call Abby hon, ever.

Instead, I swallow my bite, and say, "These are even better than the woolly mammoth burgers we had last time."

"I think I seasoned those with too much ground tusk," Cicely says.

Abby makes a strange sort of yelping sound. She folds her arms on the table, and sets her head on top. She cries.

And I:

    1. Stop eating.

    2. Study the mole on my left wrist, but only because it's difficult for me to look at Cicely's face as she's saying, "We'll find the one who did this to you." Her old smiling self's consumed by fury and grim passion once again.

    3. Wish Abby never came here.

"If he can bring your family back, we'll make him do it," Cicely says.

"I'm just so pathetic," Abby says.

I look up from my mole.

Abby's staring across the table, with her chin resting on her arm.

"Don't say that, hon," Cicely says.

Abby sniffs in some snot. "All I do is feel sorry for myself all the time," she says. "I never cry for my family at all. I don't know who they are or anything. I'm always crying for myself."

"That's OK." Cicely makes her way around the table. She rubs Abby's back, soft.

And of course I know exactly how Abby can get to know her family, even without the memories or the documents, but I don't tell her.

Because I'm:

1. Jealous.

2. Stupid.

3. Way more pathetic than she is.

"I want to do something besides cry," Abby says. "Something useful, you know? But I don't know what to do."

"Nicholas," Cicely says. "Did you bring that little notebook of yours?"

"Yeah," I say.

So during lunch, I ask Abby about her:

1. Enemies. "There's nobody I know about," she says. "But my memories are all messed up."

"What do you remember about your childhood?" Cicely says.

"Not too much." Abby picks at the edge of her Band-Aid. "In most of my memories, I'm alone, and I feel really lonely."

2. Friends. "What about people who knew you when you were a kid, like teachers? Do you remember any of them?" Cicely says.

"I don't remember any school," Abby says. "So I think I was home schooled. I remember a few family friends, and a babysitter, but none of them remember me from when I was a kid. They think we met when we were adults."

3. Family. Then I say, "Sorry," and move on to the next question.

On and on, and I feel sick adding Abby's words to my little purple notebook. I want to rip out her pages like a child.

"OK," Cicely says. "What did we find out?"

I show her the one commonality I circled.

"So we're looking for someone who despises the color green-lovers," she says.

"Do you think someone would really hurt us for something like that?" Abby says.

"I'm kidding, hon. Or maybe it's not so ridiculous a thought. Who knows how this monster thinks?"

Abby bites her fingernails.

My watch beeps.

"I'd better go," I say.

I don't want to, really. I want to stay here, wishing Abby away with the power of my mind, until my wish comes true.

"Thanks for the sandwiches," I say. And maybe I sound as doom and gloomy as I feel.

Because Cicely says, "You haven't been slapped yet today?"

I shake my head.

"Wouldn't it be better if it came from somebody who cares about you?" she says.

"I don't know," I say.

I don't want her to offer, because I'd probably say yes.

"I could do it," Abby says. "I mean, if it would help and everything."

And suddenly, I hate myself for hating this girl.

"It would help," I say. "Thank you."

"Do you want me to do it now?" she says.

I nod.

So Abby and me, we approach each other.

"It has to be hard," I say.

"Alright," she says. "Are you ready?"

I nod again.

At that, she slaps me hard. But it's not really me she's attacking. She's fighting the creature in the swirling darkness, and that's what I tell myself when I say, "Thank you."

She says, "Anytime."

After the three of us watch *The Adventures of Baron Munchausen*, I go home and:

    1. Sit down.

    2. Empty my pockets.

    3. Examine the bits and pieces of my life.

When I look at the photo of the smiling couple, all I can really think about is Abby frowning in that luscious garden, all alone.

I start to feel a little bit of Cicely's fury, maybe.

Someone rings the doorbell.

And maybe there's still some grim passion in my eyes when I open the door.

Because Karl says, "I'm sorry, man. Am I interrupting something?"

"No, it's fine," I say.

I don't say, "Come in."

"I'm sorry about the other night," Karl says. "I was stressed about the whole Heather thing. She left me for an older man. Did you know that?"

"I didn't," I say. "That sucks." As if an older man is worse than a younger man, or a man of the same age.

"And she left this message on my machine, telling me they're going on vacation to New Zealand, rubbing my face in it. Can you believe that shit?"

"No."

"Anyway, I brought you a get-well gift."

"Get-well?"

"You're such a weakling, I'm sure that slap caused a lot of damage. I'm surprised they let you out of the hospital already."

"You're hilarious."

Karl hands me the plastic bag he's been holding.

I peek inside.

"It's beer," Karl says. "Non-alcoholic, of course." He grins.

"Thanks," I say.

"Feel like a drink?"

"I'm actually waking up early tomorrow. I should go to bed soon."

Karl's smile contorts. "I come here offering you an olive branch, and you're still treating me like an asshole. What's your problem, man?"

I'm silent for a while.

I think about saying, "I don't have a problem."

But I'm feeling:

    1. Charged, because I can't get Abby's photograph out of my head.

    2. Safe, because Abby slapped me hard.

So instead, I say, "Do you know how hard it is to keep my life from falling apart? You were sober for a while, so I'm sure you know. You're a good guy, Karl, but you're not good for me. I can't have you in my home. If you decide to get help for yourself, then yeah, I'll hang out. But not before that."

Then Karl:

    1. Slaps me.

    2. Says, "Asshole."

    3. Takes back the beer.

    4. Walks away.

In other words:

    1. Abby's full-blown slap didn't count.

Or:

    2. Karl acted on his own.

But right now, it doesn't really matter.

All that matters is:

    1. My watch is beeping.

    2. It's time for bed.

#21

IN MY DREAM, Brienda's my mother. I'm trying to tell her how sorry I am that I couldn't save her, but she can't hear me. Or maybe she's ignoring me.

I notice a creature outside the window. He's watching us. He's only two slivers of eye in the swirling darkness, but he's still uglier than anything I've ever seen.

When I look back, my mother's not there.

And part of me knows she's more than missing.

She's gone.

Outside of this nightmare, awake, I escape to the living room.

"That must have been a fuck of a bad dream," Gordon says.

"How do you know that?" I say.

"I told you before. You make these freaky whimpering sounds. You were louder than normal this time."

I take my usual seat beside him. "You could wake me up if it bothers you."

"I wouldn't want to deprive you of a nightmare."

"You're a great friend."

"I'm serious. Nightmares have a bad rep, but their sole purpose is to help us and bring us closer to inner peace."

"I thought you hated the whole peace through war approach."

"Shut up, Nick. Nightmares aren't warriors. They're messengers. People should listen to them instead of shooting at them all the time."

"And what exactly are the nightmares trying to tell us?"

"It's like this. If you put your hand in a fire, you're going to feel pain, right?"

"Right."

"That pain doesn't exist to fuck with you. It's a warning sign, telling you that you need to move your hand, or things are gonna get bad. Same with nightmares. They're saying that something's burning inside you, emotionally, and you need to do something about it, or things are gonna get bad."

Maybe something is burning inside me.

Something precious.

"Alright," I say. "I'm now officially pro-nightmare. Happy?"

"Happy," Gordon says.

We pet Meta for a while.

Then Gordon says, "Why is it that you never ask me any blind questions?"

"Blind questions?" I say.

"You know. What's it like to be blind? Do you have super hearing to compensate? We were talking about nightmares, and you didn't ask me about my nightmares. Aren't you curious?"

"I'm curious."

"Then why don't you ask me?"

"I don't know."

"It's not like you're some stranger asking me an intrusive question out of the blue. You're my best friend. If you want to ask me something, you can ask me."

"Alright. Do you ever have nightmares?"

"Of course."

"What are they like?"

"Well." Gordon spends some time scratching Meta behind the ears. Then he smiles. "Here's a good one. I'm in a room, feeling the walls, trying to find a way out. There's something in here with me. Something rotten. I can't get its stench out of my nose, my mouth. Then a deep, demonic voice tells me I'm going to hell. It sounds like he's standing right next to me, but I'm too afraid to reach out and check. I keep searching for a door. Then the wall I'm feeling isn't a wall anymore. It's a face. Two strong arms wrap around me. I struggle to move, to yell, but I can't. I'm trapped. The voice growls, louder and louder. Then it's over."

"That's scary."

"You're fucking right it's scary."

"So what was that nightmare telling you?"

"At the time, I was dating this sighted girl named Pam. One night, after dinner, her mom took me aside and asked if I'd break up with Pam for Pam's sake. Apparently, she didn't think Pam could succeed in college and date someone like me at the same time."

"That's stupid."

"Yeah. The problem was, I didn't tell Pam's mom that. I'd sort of given up on standing up for myself, because no matter how hard I tried to demand respect, the world wouldn't change. After that night, I started having the nightmares. And I realized it didn't matter what the fuck other people did or didn't do. I needed to stand up for myself, for me. Otherwise, I'd be haunted by unresolved feelings of helplessness."

"Ah."

"I'm hungry as fuck. Let's move into the kitchen."

We do.

After breakfast, my watch beeps.

That means I should:

1. Get out the photo of the happy couple.

2. Draw my stencil of the severed head.

3. Use tailor's chalk to trace the stencil onto the fabric.

And I should definitely:

4. Stop thinking about Abby and her photograph.

Instead, I join Gordon on the couch again, and say, "What do you know about psychopaths?"

"A lot," Gordon says. "What do you want to know exactly?"

"I guess I want the basic profile."

"What kind of psychopath are we talking about here? A killer?"

I think of Abby's missing family. "I think so."

"A serial killer?"

"Maybe."

Gordon massages Meta's head, as if this helps him think. Maybe it does. "Most serial killers are white males, between the ages of 18 and 32. About 85% of them are American. Most of them work alone. Although work probably isn't the best word to describe it. Almost all of them suffer some kind of abuse as children, but I'm sure that's no surprise."

"Not really."

"Do you know about the MacDonald Triad?"

I:

1. Shake my head.

2. Feel stupid.

3. Say, "No."

"The Triad's made up of three behaviors that show up in many serial killers' backgrounds, at least based on limited clinical samples. These are arson, animal abuse. Usually bigger animals, like cats and dogs. And bedwetting."

"Bedwetting? That's the stupidest thing I've ever heard."

"Hey, don't shoot the messenger here."

"Sorry."

"It's bedwetting beyond the age when kids usually stop. 10 or so, I think. Anyway, like I said, the Triad's not based on a fuck-load of evidence. It's still something to think about. If a kid does this stuff, it doesn't mean he's necessarily gonna become a killer. But these may be valid warning signs."

"Fine."

"What else?" He rubs his forehead. "Most serial killers aren't psychotics. They don't hear voices or see things. They're people who've been made to feel powerless, through acts of physical and sexual dominance. So what do they do to feel powerful? They dominate others. Often times their murder rituals directly relate to their own childhood abuses. This is what I find most interesting about the whole serial killer phenomenon."

"Murder rituals?"

"The notion of dominance as power. It never really works out. The killer may start out feeling like the angel of death, choosing who lives and who dies. But he ends up feeling more powerless and out of control than ever before. Like there's something bloodthirsty and insatiable inside him. Keep in mind, I'm speaking in generalities about all this. There are always exceptions, thank god."

"What do you mean, thank god?"

"I mean. Well, life would get boring without exceptions, don't you think?"

"I guess so."

But I think I'd prefer a boring, unexceptional life any day.

I don't tell Gordon that.

Instead, I say, "How do they choose their victims?"

"For the most part, it's fairly random and opportunistic," Gordon says. "They usually don't know their victims."

"So you're saying the killers are strangers."

"Yeah."

"And this is coming from the guy who gave me a pro-stranger speech a few days ago."

"Shut up, Nick. I was saying that strangers aren't the big problem. This holds true with murders as well. You're way more likely to be killed by someone you know intimately. Anyway, I said the basic serial killer chooses his victims randomly, but that's only true to an extent. Even if there's no personal connection between him and his victims, there's probably a sort of symbolic relevance. Most likely, the victims represent someone in his past. So he may only go after a certain gender and age group. Even people with a specific haircut."

"What about people who share a favorite color?"

"As long as the detail plays an important role in his dominance fantasies, then yeah."

"Thanks for the help." I hope I don't sound sarcastic.

"Fuck, you're bailing already? We just scraped the surface."

"No offense, Gordon. I just don't want to think about this stuff anymore. At least not for a while."

"Fair enough."

But I do keep thinking about this stuff. I think about:

1. Abby's parents and brother drifting in the swirling darkness, unable to move or speak, lost in this void forever.

2. My mom screaming as a sick American asshole slices her stomach with a scalpel and sticks his hands into her guts.

Maybe:

1. This never happened to her.

2. About 90% of missing people return home.

Still, part of me knows she's more than missing.

She's gone.

As soon as I step inside Cicely's home, my eyes flick to my usual spot on the couch. Abby's not there. In fact, I don't see her at all. I:

1. Sigh with relief.

2. Feel pathetic.

"Are we having a picnic?" Cicely says, looking at my basket.

"They're muffins," I say. "Whole-grain vegan muffins, but muffins nonetheless."

"Did you bake them?"

"Nah, I'm friends with the Keebler Elves."

I don't tell her, "My step-dad's new girlfriend gave them to me on her way to work."

I don't tell her, I felt sick to my stomach when Brienda hugged me and said, "Sol told me everything. I understand."

"It's a nice day," Cicely says. "Shall we get out there and picnic?"

We picnic.

Cicely's backyard is overrun with:

1. Bamboo.

2. Weeds.

3. Stone animals.

And according to Cicely:

4. Garden sprites.

"We have to sing them a song," Cicely says. "Or else they'll keep trying to pull out our nose hairs."

"I can't sing," I say.

"Not to worry. Sprites are very forgiving creatures."

"Well. Alright."

"A round of Itsy Bitsy should do the trick. Ready?"

"Ready."

And I only feel stupid for a second.

Then I:

1. Smile.

2. Laugh.

3. Feel better.

I open up the basket.

"Muffin?" I say.

"Yes, dear?" Cicely says, and grins.

An invisible flame may be licking my face all over as I hand Cicely a muffin.

I take a bite of my own.

This is probably the best whole-grain vegan muffin I've ever tasted. The best muffin period, maybe.

But it doesn't matter.

What matters is, the muffin doesn't remind me of my mother's cooking in the least.

"These are delicious," Cicely says, with her mouth packed, obviously trying to make me laugh.

It works.

She gulps down some water. "I wonder what the secret ingredient is," she says.

"How do you know there's a secret ingredient?" I say.

"Everything this good has a secret ingredient. That's one of the 3 basic rules of the Universe."

"I must've missed that day of school. What're the other 2?"

Cicely runs her hand across the weeds beside her, as if she's petting the ground. Maybe she is. "The 2nd rule is, fresh baked bread will always smell at least a tiny bit better than it tastes."

"Alright. And the 3rd?"

She watches the ladybug trekking the back of her hand. "The 3rd rule is, love is a wonderful important thing, but it's never enough on its own." These words come out, fast and easy.

"Oh."

Cicely and me, we gaze at a small tan bird that landed nearby.

Then it flies away.

Cicely's still staring at the spot where the bird was hopping, and this makes me feel a little sad. I don't know why.

"It's nice out here," I say.

"It hasn't always been such a peaceful place," Cicely says.

"Yeah?"

"The political tension between the yard gnomes and the stone animals was on the rise for quite some time. Recently, the situation escalated into violence. That's why I have to keep the yard gnomes in the house."

"I see."

Cicely looks me in the eyes, and after a short time this becomes the longest she's ever looked me in the eyes.

Then she gasps.

And I'm sure:

1. Somehow, in my eyes, she's seen everything I've ever done.

2. She hates me.

3. She's going to slap me, hard.

I want to close my eyes.

"I thought of something," Cicely says. "A possibility."

"What?" I say.

"I was thinking about how it feels like I've known you forever."

My heart knocks on my chest. "I feel that way too."

She smiles. "Then I realized, it's possible that we have known each other forever. Well, not forever, but longer than we think."

"What do you mean?"

"Abby said the people who interacted with her when she was a child couldn't remember those experiences anymore. What if we both knew Abby and her family, and we knew each other through them? We could have talked to each other at their get-togethers over the years. That could explain our feelings."

My heart sinks a little. "I guess that's possible. But wouldn't Abby remember us?"

"The only memories she has of family friends are when she was alone with them. But maybe when we were around Abby and each other, her family was always there too, so all those memories were taken from us."

"That makes sense."

"If all this is true, then it might relate to why we were targeted and who's responsible. But it's just a theory. Maybe we've known each other for years. Maybe not. All I know for sure is that I feel a deep connection with both of you." My heart sinks a little farther, and the backyard is overrun with silence.

Then my watch beeps.

I don't remember why.

Abby:

    1. Says, out of breath, "Sorry I'm late."

    2. Wipes the sweat off her face with her sleeve.

    3. Sits down beside me, at Cicely's usual spot on the couch.

    4. Says, to me, "Did it work?"

At first I don't know what she's talking about. Then I remember, and shrug.

"I was slapped again last night," I say. "But the one who slapped me may have been acting independent of the curse."

"Do you want to try again?" Abby says.

"That'd be great." I try to smile.

"Now?"

"No time like the present."

So she stands, and I join her.

"I'll be right back," Cicely says, heading into the kitchen.

"Do you think I did something wrong last time or anything?" Abby says. "Was it too soft?"

"I don't think so," I say. "Just do what you did before."

"Alright."

And she slaps me again, without hesitation, just as hard as before.

"Thanks," I say.

"No problem," she says, sitting again.

"Here you are, hon," Cicely says, handing Abby a cup. "Fresh snowman's blood."

Abby studies the ice water for a moment, then guzzles it down.

Cicely doesn't say, "Could you move please, Abby? That's my seat."

Instead, she:

    1. Sits on the chair.

    2. Goes on to tell Abby the theory she thought of at the picnic.

All the while, Abby crunches ice cubes. Then she says, "That would mean neither of you was ever alone with me, even when I was an adult. That's sort of weird, you know?"

"Maybe we lost touch with your family when you were still a child," Cicely says.

"That's true."

"In any case, it's something to think about."

"Yeah."

"Would you like more Yeti tears?"

"What?"

"More water?"

Abby nods. "I'm really thirsty."

Cicely leaves with Abby's cup.

Abby looks me in the eyes, as if she's going to tell me something important. Then she bursts into tears.

"What's wrong?" I say, and I feel stupid for saying it.

She leans forward, crying into her palms.

And I feel sorry for:

    1. Her.

But also:

    2. Myself.

This combination is strong enough that it almost floods out in tears.

"I'm sorry," I say, meaning I'm:

    1. Not only sorry for her loss.

    2. Apologizing for wishing her gone.

With plenty of hesitation, I put my arm around her.

Then she:

    1. Turns to face me.

2. Wraps her arms around me.

3. Buries her face.

Cicely sets the cup down on the table in front of us, and says, "I'll go get dinner ready." She leaves us alone.

I pat Abby's back, gentle and awkward, with one hand.

After a while, she:

1. Releases me.

2. Wipes her face with her sleeve.

3. Says, "Sorry about your shirt. I got it all snotty."

"It's alright," I say.

She sips from her cup.

"I sort of know how you feel," I say. "My mom disappeared too, years ago."

"She did?" Abby says.

"Not in the same way as yours, of course. I can still remember her."

"Oh. You're lucky."

"Yeah, real lucky." I hope I sound sarcastic.

"I'd give anything for just one memory of them. Just something to hold onto, you know? I'd even be happy with a sad memory. Is that crazy?"

My empathy wins over again. "I don't think so."

She sips more water. "I know remembering them would make things worse for me in some ways. I'd feel the pain of losing real people, but I think that's better than feeling like I've always been really lonely."

"I think you're right." I take a deep breath. "Abby, I think there's a way you can get to know your family on some level, even without the memories or photographs."

"What do you mean?"

"Well, you grew up with them, and they loved you. I'm sure they left deep impressions in you that help make up who you are. I don't think anyone can take that away from you."

"How do you know that?"

"I don't know. I guess it's just a feeling."

A fairy tale sort of feeling, but a feeling nonetheless.

Cicely pops her head into the doorway. "Shall we dine?" she says.

We dine.

"This is delicious," I say. "What is it?"

Though I already know it's falafel.

"Pita and fried sea monster earwax," Cicely says. "I'm boiling the eyeballs for dessert. It's a delicacy in Atlantis."

"I thought Atlantis was lost," I say.

"It was, for a while. Then it turned up in New Jersey a few months ago."

"Oh."

We go on like this for most of the dinner, and Abby turns her head back and forth as we speak.

Then Cicely stops talking for a while. She taps the tennis ball against the table, over and over.

Finally, she says, "Abby, if my theory about us is the truth, then it's possible Nicholas and I spent time with your family friends when we visited you and your parents. It might help if we met these friends."

"You think you can figure out if your theory's true or not by meeting them?" Abby says.

"There's no way to be sure, but we can at least see if they feel familiar to us. It's not evidence exactly, but it's something."

"That's true."

"How about I host a dinner party tomorrow, or someday soon. You can tell one of those family friends that I want you to bring a guest. Do you think that would work?"

"I think so. Who should I invite?"

"Any of them. I'd like to get to know all of them eventually."

"Alright."

I see a glimmer of grim passion in Cicely's eyes, and I know:

1. The reason Cicely gave isn't the real reason she wants to meet these family friends.

2. Strangers aren't the big problem in this world. So the person who cursed us is most likely someone we know, or at least knew, intimately.

In other words, Cicely's not throwing a party.

She's setting a trap.

There's a man in a dark suit leaning against my car. The streetlight's somewhat dim, so I can't tell who he is until I'm close.

By then, it's too late to hide.

"What's your name?" John says.

"Nicholas," I say, and set my basket on the car.

"You shouldn't have punched me, Nicholas. But I should've turned the other cheek. I'm ashamed of what I did. I'm sorry."

I flinch when he holds out his hand.

"Please accept my apology," he says.

I shake his hand.

John sighs and says, "Ever since I've known Cissy, she's driven me crazy. I used to like that feeling. But now it's like she's turning me into someone I'm not. Do you know what I mean?"

I:

    1. Shrug.

    2. Try to examine the mole on my left wrist, but I need more light.

"Has she told you about the tennis ball?" he says.

"Yeah," I say.

"I can't tell you how many hours I spent trying to help her see reason, but she refused." He runs his hands down his face. "She's always had a problem facing reality. I should've seen this coming." He laughs. "But how could I? It's nuts."

I pull my keys out of my pocket.

"So, Nicholas," John says, eyeing me now. "How long have you two been seeing each other?"

"We're friends," I say.

"Don't worry. I'm just curious. I don't want her back." He laughs again.

Suddenly, I:

    1. Stop thinking about how John attacked me.

    2. Start thinking about how John attacked Cicely.

3. Squeeze my keys.

"It's really none of your business," I say.

"I'm her husband, Nicholas," John says. "The least you can do is tell me the truth."

The least I can do is get in my car, slam the door, and speed away.

Instead, I say, "The truth is, you need to stop stalking Cicely and get some professional help."

He:

1. Shoots a sharp laugh at my face.

But it's not enough, apparently, because then he:

2. Slaps me hard.

And I know:

1. Abby's full-blown slap didn't count.

2. When she slapped me, she was acting out of compassion.

3. This curse isn't about compassion.

"You're just as crazy as she is," John says, and he gets in his car, slams the door, and speeds away.

I don't follow in hot pursuit.

I don't want to be Batman.

What I do is return to Cicely's house, and tell her what happened.

She:

1. Touches my cheek, soft.

2. Says, "I'm sorry."

I don't say anything. I just swallow.

"We'll figure out who did this to us," she says. "We'll make him undo what he did."

"Yeah," I say, and I almost believe her.

For now, that's enough.

#22

IF CICELY'S THEORY is correct, then:

    1. This elderly woman, Kin, could be the one responsible for our curses.

    2. This could be an earth-shattering, epic dinner.

But my mind refuses to stay focused on these 2 disturbing possibilities. Because if Cicely's theory is correct, it also means:

    3. Cicely and I didn't meet for the first time when I was outside this house, scraping flecks of old paint off the wall. She didn't offer me a glass of "iceberg juice" and I didn't chuckle. Our conversation didn't surge from there, fast and easy. This wasn't the first and only time in my life where I felt so comfortable with a stranger that I didn't glance at my watch or my mole once. On my drive home, I didn't think the word "magical." We didn't happen to meet in the supermarket a few days later, and after our time together, she didn't say, "Shall we meet up next week? Same bat time? Same bat channel?" I didn't beam at her the way I hadn't beamed at anyone since before my mother disappeared.

My thoughts scatter when Kin says, "Is your boyfriend always so quiet, Abby?"

"I'm not her boyfriend," I say.

"He's my friend," Abby says.

I didn't know I was her friend.

"You'd make a beautiful couple," Kin says, and turns to Cicely. "Wouldn't they?"

"They are beautiful," Cicely says.

I stare at my burrito.

"So, what is it you do, Nicholas?" Kin says.

"I make stuffed animals," I say.

"Isn't that wonderful? Bringing joy to children's hearts."

"Actually, most of my customers are adults. I shouldn't say stuffed animals, because I make stuffed whatever-my-customers-want. Baseballs, presidents, eggplants."

"Oh! Crafting toys for the children in all of us. The world would be a much better place if there were more people like you. No doubt about that."

I can't think of anything else to say but, "Thanks."

"Could you make me a stuffed ant?" Abby says. "I'll pay for it and everything."

The truth is, I:

1. Don't want to make a plush for Abby before I make one for Cicely.

2. Still haven't thought of the perfect plush for Cicely, though the stuffed Terry Gilliam sitting on a stuffed director's chair might be the best I can come up with.

Still, I say, "Alright."

"You don't have to make it look cute," Abby says. "I mean, sometimes people change how animals look when they make them into toys, so that they're cuter, but I already think ants are cute on their own. I don't mean the toy has to be ant-sized or anything. Just the details can stay the same, you know?"

"Got it."

Abby grins. "Thanks, Nick."

I wince. "You're welcome."

"Leave it to Abby to find the beauty in bugs," Kin says, and laughs. "You're a darling girl, do you know that?"

Abby looks down at her plate, blushing.

"How did you two meet?" Cicely says, to Kin.

"It must have been 2 years ago," Kin says. "We met at the pet store where Abby worked. I was buying a rabbit. We talked, and of course I realized she was the sweetest young lady in the world, so I left her with my phone number. We've been friends ever since."

Cicely:

1. Smiles at Kin.

   2. Gives Abby the signal, by scratching her nose.

Hours ago, Cicely told Abby exactly what to say. When Abby asked why, Cicely said, "It might help." And Abby didn't ask any more questions.

   "Oh, I almost forgot to tell you all," Abby says. "My parents are coming to visit me next week."

   Of course, Cicely's staring at Kin to catch her reaction.

I'm watching Kin too, and I see her eyes and mouth crinkle with a big grin.

   "It would be great if we could all get together sometime next week," Abby says.

   "I'd love to meet them," Kin says. "They must be lovely people, to raise such a lovely daughter."

   I hear Cicely sigh.

   Then Kin turns to Cicely and says, "I wouldn't usually say this, but I can see how important this is to you. I'm not the person you're looking for, Cicely."

   Cicely's eyes widen.

   "But I may be able to help you find him," Kin says. "I believe it's a him anyway."

   "What're you talking about?" Abby says.

   "Cicely thought I may have been the one who hurt all of you," Kin says. "I'm sure she had good reason. She's a very smart woman."

   Abby bites her fingernails.

   "How do you know all this?" Cicely says, with more than a little grim passion in her eyes.

   "Your feelings are so strong," Kin says. "I couldn't help but know."

   "You read her mind?" Abby says. "I didn't know you could do that."

   "I'm sorry I never told you," Kin says. "I have a difficult time not feeling responsible for the people I share this with. It's the mother in me, I suppose. So I try to keep the skill to myself, if I can help it. But I couldn't ignore what's happening here. If there's a chance I can help you find this man, I have to try."

   "How?" Cicely says.

   "I need to touch something that he's touched," Kin says.

   After a few moments of silence, Cicely:

   1. Lifts her hand up from under the table.

    2. Looks at the tennis ball.

And I'm sure she knows, Kin could be:

    1. Acting.

    2. The one responsible for our curses.

Then again, Kin could have kept quiet about knowing anything, and she would have seemed a lot less suspicious.

Maybe this is what Cicely's thinking.

Maybe not.

What matters is, Cicely:

    1. Stands.

    2. Walks over to Kin's side.

    3. Says, "You can touch it, but don't take it out of my hand."

"I wouldn't dream of it," Kin says, and smiles.

I make my way over to Cicely's side.

Cicely holds out the tennis ball. "OK," she says.

"You have beautiful fingernails," Kin says.

"Thank you," Cicely says.

Kin:

    1. Reaches out.

    2. Touches the tennis ball.

    3. Closes her eyes.

The only sound I can hear is Abby tapping her fingers against the table.

Finally, Kin opens her eyes and says, "No. No. No!"

Cicely pulls the tennis ball away.

Kin stands. "No!" she says.

Cicely backs away, holding the tennis ball against her chest.

I just stand there.

Kin:

    1. Looks me in the face.

    2. Says, "No!"

And I'm afraid somehow she's seen everything I've ever done.

    3. Slaps me.

4. Vomits burrito all over my shirt.

5. Collapses to the floor.

"Kin!" Abby says.

For some reason, I lift Kin back to her chair.

"I need to sit down," Kin says.

"You are sitting," Abby says.

"Should I call an ambulance?" Cicely says.

"I'll be fine," Kin says. "I just need to rest here a minute."

"I'll get you a washcloth," Cicely says, and leaves the room.

"Your poor shirt," Kin says, looking at me. "I'll buy you a new one."

"It's alright," I say. "I'm sure it'll wash out."

"No, I feel terrible," Kin says. "Tell me where you bought it, and I'll buy you a new one tomorrow."

"I bought it from a thrift store for a few dollars," I say. "I don't even like this shirt."

Kin smiles. "You're a sweet boy."

Cicely returns with:

1. A washcloth.

2. Two t-shirts.

She gives the washcloth to Kin, and holds out the shirts to me. "This one's John's," she says, lifting up the plain white one. "But I wasn't sure if you'd want to wear one of his, so I brought one of mine too."

"Thanks," I say, and change into the t-shirt with the dancing cactuses on the front.

Cicely and me, we return to our seats.

"What did you see?" Abby says.

"I saw a little girl with her mouth filled with maggots," Kin says.

"We have to help her," Abby says. "Where is she?"

"There is no little girl," Kin says. "I always see her and the maggots when I connect with a situation like this. The feeling I got was a lot stronger than I've ever felt before."

"Do you know where he is?" Cicely says.

"I don't know where he is, or what he is," Kin says.

"Do you know why he did this to us?" Cicely says.

"I only know what he's capable of." Kin places the washcloth on her plate, and looks Cicely in the eyes. "You're a strong and caring woman, Cicely. That's a blessing, certainly, but God knows it's not always easy. I spent most of my life trying to save everyone around me. I failed, of course, and I was miserable and lonely. That only changed when I learned when to stop fighting and let go."

Cicely gives Kin a look that says I'm-not-going-to-let-go.

"This isn't a fight you can win," Kin says. "The closer you get to the truth, the more you're going to suffer. I wish I had better news. I'm sorry."

"Do you know what this man did to us?" Cicely says.

Kin shakes her head.

"He took Abby's family away," Cicely says.

"I thought they were visiting next week," Kin says.

"That was a lie. We don't know where they are. Can you help us look for them?"

"Of course."

"I don't have anything they touched," Abby says. "I don't know what they touched."

"They've given you plenty of affection, I'm sure," Kin says. "Give me your hands, and I'll take a look."

Abby and Kin, they join hands.

"You don't have to squeeze so tight, dear," Kin says.

"Sorry," Abby says.

Then Kin:

    1. Closes her eyes.

    2. Takes a deep breath.

    3. Opens her eyes.

    4. Says, "I'm sorry. I can't see them."

"What does that mean?" Abby says, pulling her hands away.

"They're hidden from me," Kin says. "It doesn't mean that they're gone. They could be alive and well somewhere. I'm sure they are."

"I hope so," Abby says.

Kin looks at her watch. "Where has the time gone?" She stands. "Thank you for the wonderful dinner, Cicely. It was a pleasure to meet you. And you too, Nicholas. Such a handsome young man."

"Nice to meet you," I say.

"I'll drive you home," Abby says.

"Thank you for the help," Cicely says.

"I only wish I could do more," Kin says.

"I'll be back soon," Abby says.

Abby and Kin, they head for the door.

But I can't let go.

"Wait," I say, and approach Kin. "My mom went missing years ago. We don't know what happened to her. Could you…"

Kin holds out her hands.

I take them.

Then Kin:

1. Closes her eyes.

2. Takes a deep breath.

3. Removes her hands.

4. Says, "I'm sorry. I only see the girl."

I imagine my mom gagging, her throat packed with squirming maggots.

"It doesn't mean she's passed on," Kin says. "It only means that your separation from her is out of your control. I'm sure she's fine."

I don't say, "How could you possibly know that?"

I don't say, "I'm sure she's dead."

Instead, I say, "Thank you."

After Abby and Kin leave, I take my spot on the couch.

Cicely, hers.

She:

1. Touches my arm, soft.

2. Says, "I'm so sorry about your mother."

And she doesn't say, with fury in her forehead:

1. "We'll find her."

2. "We'll save her."

3. "We'll bring her home."

"Do you think Kin's the one who cursed us?" I say.

"The Magic 8-Ball in my gut says 'don't count on it,'" Cicely says. "Then again, I asked it about John years ago, and it said 'outlook good.'"

I smile a little.

"In any case, Kin's probably right about how dangerous this fight is," Cicely says, and her gaze touches mine. "But I'm going to keep fighting."

"I know," I say.

"Of course, this may be the stupidest decision of my life, and I'd understand if you wanted to make a different one."

"Nah, I wouldn't want to give up the benefits of being in the Cicely army. There's great food, great movies, great company. A lot of greats."

"I didn't know I had an army."

"Well, an army of yard gnomes."

"You mean they let you join? I'm surprised. The last time I checked they were extremely xenophobic."

"They still are, I think. I just happen to be a gnome."

"A giant gnome?"

"There are more of us than you think."

Our conversation surges on, fast and easy.

And maybe this is a mistake, trying to discover the identity of a sick and powerful bastard who gets off on fucking with people's lives, so that we can:

1. Find him.

2. Face him.

3. Bring him down.

I can't see that turning out well, but it doesn't matter.

This is still the best mistake I've ever made.

By far.

#23

IN MY DREAM, Kin's a psychopathic bride. I'm trying to tell her how sorry I am that I didn't listen to her, but she can't hear me. Or maybe she's ignoring me.

I notice a head outside the window. It's watching us. It's ugly, with blood erupting from its mouth, but it's still mine.

Then the bride's body contorts. Her head sinks into her chest and she yanks at her hair and screams for help. But it's no use.

I can't even save myself.

Outside of this nightmare, awake, I escape to my workstation on the floor.

And the happy couple in the photograph becomes:

1. A gag gift.

Or:

2. Part of a morbid toy collection.

Or:

3. Revenge.

It doesn't really matter what it's for.

What matters is that I:

1. Finish it.

2. Seal it.

3. Mail it.

And that's exactly what I do.

Then I join Gordon and Meta on the couch.

"So, you want to know more about killers," Gordon says.

"How do you know that?" I say, thinking back to Kin.

"You fart when you're nervous."

"No I don't."

"It's nothing to be ashamed of, Nick. The mind-body connection is a beautiful thing."

"Shut up."

"Alright. Let's talk about killers then. What do you want to know?"

"I'm not sure. You decide."

"Well." Gordon runs his hand through his hair. "If you really want to understand the mind of a serial killer, you should know most of them don't wake up one morning and decide, 'Hey, I think murder is my cup of tea.' They don't suddenly snap, I mean. Many of them start fantasizing about killing people when they're teenagers, or even before that. And when these behaviors of dominance cross over to reality, many aspects of the fantasy tend to cross over with them. Like the killer may fantasize about gagging women with their underwear, so that's what he does in real life. Of course, fantasy and reality are very different animals. He'll feel powerful and in control in his fantasy world, but then when he actually kills for the first time, he'll probably feel ashamed, disgusted, afraid, you name it."

"If that's true, then why does he keep doing it?"

"I told you before. This is about power. He'll feel powerful terrifying his victim and getting away with murder. Afterward, he'll relive these feelings by revisiting the crime scene, or looking at the trophy he took from his victim, or watching the videotape of the actual murder, or just fantasizing about what happened. For the serial killer, fantasy bleeds into reality, and reality bleeds into fantasy. But no matter how much bleeding goes on, he'll never become the god he imagines himself to be. More and more, he'll become a slave to his own impulses. It'd be poetic, if it wasn't so tragic and fucked up."

"Yeah."

"I smell another fart. Do you want me to stop?"

"No. Keep going. Some of this might help."

Gordon touches his chin, the way he does when he's nervous. "What do you mean help?"

"Nothing. It doesn't matter."

"Why are you asking me about killers, Nick? I thought this was a bonding thing. Showing an interest in my passion. But that's not it, is it?"

"Fine, you caught me. I'm looking to murder somebody and I'm trying to learn the ins and outs."

Gordon snorts. "Right. Weren't you the guy last night who was saying, 'Sorry, Mr. Spider, but I have to take you outside. I'm sure you'll find a nice Mrs. Spider to settle down with. Everything's gonna be alright.'"

"What's your point?"

"I want to know what this is really about."

"You wouldn't believe me."

"Maybe I will, maybe I won't. What I do know is that I'll try my damnedest to understand you. That's what's really important, isn't it?"

"I guess so."

"Alright then. What's this all about?"

Part of me wants to:

    1. Lie to Gordon.

    2. Pretend that I live a boring, unexceptional life.

Then again, I want Gordon to be more than my best friend right now. I want him to be my doorway out of this nightmare.

So I say, "Someone's been fucking with my life. I don't know who he is, or how he's doing what he's doing. I don't know how to find him, and I don't know how to stop him if I do."

"And you think this guy is a serial killer?" Gordon says.

"Maybe. I'm not sure yet."

"Have you gone to the police?"

"I don't think they're taking on many curse cases these days."

"Curse? Is this connected with that slapping thing you told me about?"

"Yeah."

"Nick," Gordon says, soft, and rubs his chin. "I know this guy seems real, but there's no one after you. You're gonna have to trust me about that. This is about you and your fear."

"Yeah. I'm afraid he's gonna turn me into a rabbit and stomp me to death."

"Nick, you're afraid that you deserve to be punished. You haven't dealt with these feelings, and they're powerful, so they've built up over the years and manifested as a powerful figure. But he only exists in your head."

"He's real."

"Have you ever seen him?"

"I don't have to see him to know he's real. I've seen what he's done to people."

"So he's hurt more than just you?"

"That's what I'm saying, Gordon. He cursed two friends of mine, on exactly the same day that he cursed me, so I know it's not just in my head."

"Do you have any evidence that he hurt these friends on the same day?"

"Not exactly. They told me."

"And how do you know they're not trying to validate their own delusions?"

"So you're saying we're all delusional."

"I'm not trying to insult you, Nick. I'm trying to help you see the real problem, so that you can deal with it."

"If you really want to help me, tell me what to do when I'm confronting a psychopath."

"That won't help you."

I stand. "I'll be back later tonight."

Gordon sighs. "Spending time with these people is only gonna make the killer and the curse seem that much more real. You'll rationalize each other like crazy. I can give you perspective."

"I don't want any more of your perspective right now."

"Just one more thing, Nick. You said I slapped you that night during your experiment, but I remember punching you. How do you know you're not remembering it as a slap to feed the fantasy?"

"How do you know you're not the one remembering it wrong?"

"Maybe I am and maybe I'm not. That's the fucking point. Memories are about as reliable as my eyeballs. OK, that's overstating the fact, but you should check out the research on this stuff. You'd be surprised what deceitful little bastards memories can be."

I head for the door. "I'm going."

"You want to know how to stop this killer? Forgive yourself, and he'll disappear from your life forever."

"Thanks. I'll be sure to do that."

And I know:

1. This is almost the same conversation I've had with myself many times before.
2. Gordon's only trying to help.

But it doesn't matter.

I:

1. Say, "See you later."
2. Step outside.
3. Close the door.

I don't want to, really. I want to go back inside and believe Gordon's words, like a child believing in a fairy tale, and I want to escape this nightmare forever.

But I can't.

I realize now that it's easy to tell the difference between a real problem and an imaginary one.

It's just the terror of facing the truth that's hard.

When I return from the bathroom, Abby's saying, "But Kin said you can't beat him. She said you'd only suffer."

"And I appreciate her concern," Cicely says. "But it's not up to Kin to decide what I'm capable of."

Abby looks over at me with eyes that say, "Help me."

I look away, and check my:

1. Watch.
2. Mole.
3. Pockets.

"I don't want you to get hurt because of me," Abby says.

"You're not responsible for my actions, hon," Cicely says.

"But you're only doing this because of what he did to my family. I think if you weren't so angry about that, you wouldn't still want to fight him."

"I am angry about what he did to your family, and I'm going to do everything I can to bring them back, but I'd be doing this even if we never met. If I don't hold this man accountable for what he's done, no one will."

"What if he's not a man?"

"It doesn't matter what he is. He violated me, and you, and Nicholas, and he's going to have to answer for that." She holds Abby's left hand. The one with the missing thumb. "I won't hold it against you if you don't help me. I'm doing this, with or without you."

Abby stares into Cicely's eyes, as her lower lip trembles like a child.

Maybe she believes, the way I do, that:

1. The creature in the swirling darkness is real and more than likely a killer.
2. It's only a matter of time before Cicely finds him.

And maybe these terrifying thoughts, combined with every other terrifying thought Abby's had to deal with since her curse began, floods out of her in tears.

"Please," Abby says, crackles. "I already lost too many people."

Cicely holds her. "I'll be careful."

"What if that's not enough?"

"I'll be there with her," I say, and take a seat in the chair beside them. "I can't promise I'll be the best sidekick in the world, but I do look good in tights and a cape."

Abby doesn't:

1. Laugh.
2. Smile.
3. Feel any better, I'm sure.

"Cicely and me, we'll be fine," I say. "You don't have to be a part of this anymore. You've gone through enough already."

"No," Abby says. "I mean, I'm scared and everything, but if I can't convince you to change your minds, I want to help."

"Great," Cicely says, and smiles. "I think the next step is to invite over another one of your family friends. Preferably a man, in case Kin's right about the perpetrator being one."

"I don't remember any men. Only Kin and some other women."

"Then it may be a man related to one of them. Or Kin could be wrong, and it's one of the women. Or it could be someone completely outside of this circle. But we have to start somewhere."

"That's true. I'll ask Maria. She was my babysitter."

"Thank you."

"I really don't think she did it though. I don't think any of them did it. They were always so nice to me, you know?"

"I'm sure you're right, hon. But if it is one of these women, she could have erased bad memories, and left only good ones. We know the perpetrator's capable of manipulations like that. So we'd better check them out, just in case."
Abby nods.

"That's settled then." Cicely stands. "I'll cook us some dinner. I was thinking fresh baked brownies. Then we could have some leftover pie for dessert."

"Aren't brownies already dessert?" I say.

"I'm talking about the tiny elf creatures who like to help out around the house."

"Oh. But if they're helpful, why would we eat them?"

"Because these ones died of old age, and they consider being eaten as one of the best ways to be put to rest."

"Alright then. Can I help you cook them?"

"I'm not sure. Can you cook?"

"Well, I can't promise I'll be the best sous chef in the world, but I look good in an apron."

"Then let's get cooking, shall we?"

I stand.

"I'm just gonna stay here and think for a while, if that's alright," Abby says.

"Of course," Cicely says.

So Cicely and me, we get cooking in the kitchen.

She:

    1. Places an apron with ninja carrots over my head.

    2. Ties the strings.

3. Stands back.

4. Eyes me.

5. Says, "You're right. You do look good."

I laugh a little.

"Now when do I get to see you in the tights and cape you were talking about?" she says.

"Actually those were destroyed in a fire," I say. "I burned them. I can still use my powers though."

"Good. I for one feel better knowing I have a giant gnome super hero on my side."

"No, I'm the sidekick. You're the hero."

"I don't think so, hon. I don't have any super powers. Well, I suppose I can do this." She juggles some potatoes with one hand.

"You have a lot of powers."

A swarm of ideas buzz in my mind.

I don't say, "You can transform pillows into flaming marshmallows."

I don't say, "You can make baby chimeras rain from the sky."

What I do say is, "You're a really good person."

"I don't think that counts as a super power," she says. "But thank you, Nicholas."

We get to work chopping vegetables.

Moments later, I hear a woman shout, "Nick."

And I'm sure:

1. Somehow, she knows all my secrets.

2. She hates me.

3. She's going to slap me, hard.

I want to close my eyes.

Instead, I turn around and watch as Abby:

1. Rushes close to me, smiling.

2. Stops suddenly.

3. Yelps.

4. Slaps me.

5. Looks at me with I-don't-know-what-got-into-me eyes.

And me, I don't:

1. Move.

2. Let go of the knife sticking in Abby's stomach.

3. Race for the phone.

In other words, I don't save her.

I can't even save myself.

#24

IN MY DREAM, Abby's my soul mate. I'm trying to tell her how sorry I am that I murdered her, but she can't hear me. Or maybe she's ignoring me.

No one exists outside the window.

Then my soul mate's body contorts. Her stomach ruptures and growls and forms a gaping fanged maw.

I can't hide.

Outside of this nightmare, awake, I escape to the hospital.

I don't want to, really. I want to hide in the swirling darkness with Abby's family, where I couldn't hurt anyone ever again.

But I can't.

I:

1. Glance at Cicely as she sleeps in a chair, the tennis ball in a cocoon of duct tape around her hand.
2. Approach Abby's bed.
3. Force away the memories of my own hospitalizations, so that I can focus.

Before I can get any words out, Abby says, "I'm real sorry, Nick."

I almost laugh. Instead, I say, "You don't have anything to be sorry about."

"I slapped you."

"I stabbed you with a knife."

"I ran into your knife like an idiot, then I slapped you for it."

"You've slapped me before."

"Yeah, but this was different, you know? You didn't ask me to. My body just reacted, and I hurt you. I can't stop thinking about it."

A tear rolls down her cheek, and part of me wants to hold her.

The other part of me says, "You only slapped me because of the curse."

"It doesn't matter why," she says. "I'm just really sorry."

"Abby, please stop apologizing."

"Accept my apology and I will."

I sigh. "Alright, I accept your apology. Now can I have a turn?"

"No."

"What do you mean, no?"

"You don't need to apologize. Everything was totally my fault."

I bite at my fingernail. "When you came at me, I could've let go of the knife. But I held on even tighter. I was scared, I guess. I didn't know it was you. I'm sorry."

Abby studies my face for a while then says, "It's alright."

I place the gift on her bed.

"What's this?" she says.

"I worked on it most of the night," I say.

She:

> 1. Tears at the wrapping paper.
> 2. Beams.
> 3. Says, "My ant!"
> 4. Scrambles off the bed.

"What are you doing!" I say. "You're gonna hurt yourself."

She hugs me.

I hug her back, soft.

"How much do I owe you?" she says.

"Abby—" I say.

"I'm just kidding. Thanks, Nick. He's really great." She returns to the bed, and sits there, hugging the ant.

"Have the doctors said anything new?"

"No, just that everything still looks good. It wasn't a bad stabbing at all."

"It wasn't a good stabbing either."

"Yeah, that's true."

The moment I stabbed her flashes in my head again, and as easy as it is to blame myself for that moment, I know:

1. I'm only doing so out of force of habit.
2. It's possible the curse brought about the stabbing so that Abby would slap me, and even if I somehow prevented this tragedy, something else would've happened, and someone else would've slapped me.

The only way to put a stop to these catastrophes is to discover the identity of the creature in the swirling darkness, so that we can:

1. Find him.
2. Face him.
3. Bring him down.

In other words, I can't hide.

In my dream, Abby's the little sister I never had. I'm trying to tell her how sorry I am that I called her all those horrible names, but the room shatters, and I open my eyes.

Cicely's standing over me, surrounded by white. "Abby's gone," she says.

"What?" I say.

"I woke up and she's gone." There's panic in her voice that I'm sure has everything to do with a monster who can make people disappear.

I:

1. Approach the bed.
2. Notice the note.
3. Pick it up.

"Thank god," Cicely says.

"Dear Cicely and Nick," I say. "They said I don't need to be observed anymore, and I can go home. I don't want to wake you guys up, because you look so peaceful, like sleeping babies. I'll see you later. Love, Abby."

"I can't believe they discharged her already."

"I'm sure she'll be alright." I force the note into my pocket, with all the other bits and pieces of my life.

And Cicely, she begins to unravel the duct tape from her hand.

"I'd understand if you don't want me over at your house anymore," I say.

"Because of the stabbing thing?" Cicely says.

"That, and I haven't bathed in a few weeks."

She takes my hand. "You're a really good person, Nicholas. A little stabbing isn't going to change that."

"Thanks."

"Shall we return to the bat cave?"

We return.

Abby enters the kitchen when we're preparing sandwiches.

I:

1. Make sure I'm not holding anything in my hands.

2. Turn around.

Abby looks pale.

"Are you feeling ill, hon?" Cicely says.

"Yeah, but not because of my stomach or anything," Abby says. "I'm really worried, you know?"

"I can go if you'd feel more comfortable," I say.

"No." Abby shakes her head. "I'm not worried because of you. I mean, not because you stabbed me. I just have this bad feeling in my legs. I'm afraid the monster's gonna hurt us."

"The sooner we find him, the better," Cicely says. "Did you call your babysitter?"

Abby nods. "She didn't want to come over. I called all the other women and they didn't want to come over either. What do we do?"

"We'll figure something out."

"I think I'm gonna lie down on the couch."

"I'll bring you a sandwich in a few minutes."

Abby gives a faint smile, then heads into the living room.

Cicely and me, we look at each other.

Maybe she's thinking what I'm thinking, that:

1. Only yesterday, Abby was strongly opposed to us continuing our search for the creature.

2. She could be lying about the babysitter and the other women.

Before either of us have a chance to speak, Abby returns from the living room, holding her ant.

"Could one of you come sit with me?" Abby says. "I'm sort of, you know, scared."

"I'll finish up the sandwiches," Cicely says.

So I:

  1. Follow Abby into the living room.

  2. Sit on the chair beside the couch.

Then I check my:

  1. Watch.

  2. Mole.

  3. Pockets.

"I feel stupid," Abby says, lying on the couch.

"What? Why?" I say.

"I'm like a little kid, making you come in here because I'm afraid. You must think I'm crazy."

"I don't, and I'm not just saying that because I stabbed you."

She laughs. "You're just being funny."

"No, I really do understand. I've been having a lot of nightmares recently, and every time I wake up, it's like some of the nightmare is still there in the room with me. So I get out of there as fast as I can."

"Really?"

"Yeah. And to be honest, I'm more afraid of the creature who cursed us than I am of my nightmares."

"You don't seem very scared."

"Well, I am. Though I guess I feel a lot safer when I'm over here."

"Because of Cicely?"

I feel myself swallow. "Yeah."

Abby marches the stuffed ant across her legs. "Do you really think she'll be able to stop the monster?"

"Maybe."

"But the monster has all sorts of powers. What if he can snap his fingers and make our heads blow up?"

"I don't know. But if anyone can stop him, Cicely can."

"She's just one human being, Nick."

Cicely enters the room with a platter and a smile, saying, "Who wants sphinx sandwiches?"

I raise my hand.

Maybe Cicely is just one human being.

But maybe that's enough.

At the gas station, a man in a cowboy hat:

1. Smiles at me.

2. Approaches me.

3. Says, "Nickels. How long has it been?"

"I don't know," I say.

He takes off his hat and rubs his hair. "I know you're fearing for your life right about now, but I'm not the same sort of man I used to be. I'm more forgiving. All I want is an apology."

I clear my throat. "I'm sorry."

He puts his hat back on. "You're gonna have to do better than that."

"I'm really sorry."

"I want to know what exactly you're sorry for. You wronged me more than once, if you remember."

"I'm really sorry about everything, but I have to go," I say.

He:

1. Slaps me.

2. Looks at his hand, with those I-don't-know-what-got-into-me eyes.

3. Says, "Christ, Nickels. I just fucking regressed because of you. Fuck."

4. Walks away.

And I let him go.

I don't want to, really. I want to run after him and apologize for every moment of pain I caused, even if it takes all night, so that I can forgive myself a little more.

But I can't.

I recognize the cowboy's:

    1. Voice

    2. Face.

I don't remember:

    1. His name.

    2. How I know him.

    3. Anything else.

If Gordon's right, and I've subconsciously constructed my own personal road to redemption, I don't think I'll ever make it home again.

#25

TODAY, I WAKE up to a nightmare.

On the answering machine:

1. Greg says, "I don't know what you were on last night, but if you ever speak to my wife that way again, I'm going to kill you. I'm not kidding around. Stay away from my family."

2. Sol says, "You shouldn't have said what you said, Nicholas. Brienda listened to the message before I did. I wish she never had to hear you that way. I told her that you're a different person when you drink, but she's afraid of you. And if I'm going to be honest with you, Nicholas, I'm afraid too. The things you said. I've never heard you say such terrible things. I hope you understand that Brienda and I don't want you in our home until you get help. I love you, son."

3. I say, "Hey Gordon. I feel bad about what happened between us yesterday. You called me crazy, which I find ironic, considering that you're a fucking cripple who jacks off every night thinking about serial killers. Now let me give you a little perspective. The reason you can't get a date isn't because you're blind and people don't like that. You're just so fucking ugly, no one in their right mind would—"

I delete the message.

Gordon steps into the living room. "Did you say something, Nick?"

"Did you listen to the messages yet?" I say, fast.

"No. I just woke up. Hence the pajamas."

"Do you remember what I did here last night?"

"You worked on some plush art. Then you went to sleep."

"You don't remember anything else?"

He rubs his eyes. "Well, I remember you avoiding me, but I'm guessing that's not what you're worrying about."

"Gordon, I'm—"

The theme song from *CSI* interrupts me.

"Is that my phone in your room?" Gordon says.

"I don't know," I say.

"Did you borrow it?"

"I don't know."

We head into the room, but the music stops before we can pinpoint the location.

"I'll call from the house phone," Gordon says.

I stare at my mole until the music starts up again. The sound seems to be coming from:

1. Under my bed.

And more specifically:

2. The sumo wrestler under my bed.

And even more specifically:

3. The sumo wrester's stomach.

"Did you find it?" Gordon says.

"I think so," I say.

"What do you mean?"

"I need some scissors."

I:

1. Make my way to my workstation on the living room floor.

2. Cut open the crude stitches on the sumo's stomach.

3. Stick my shaking hand into his polyfil guts.

4. Pull out the phone.

5. Check the dialed calls from last night.

Starting at about 1AM, someone called:

1. Sol.

2. Karl.

3. Nadia.

4. The house phone here.

I don't see Cicely's number listed, so a small wave of relief ripples in my gut.

"Here," I say, crackle, and hand over the phone. "Sorry about that."

"Are you alright?" Gordon says.

"I don't think so."

"Do you want to talk about it?"

I don't say, "Not with you."

Instead, I say, "I'm sorry about avoiding you. I know you only wanted to help."

"Jesus fuck, Nick," Gordon says. "How many times are you gonna apologize after I disrespect you? I have no right to force advice on anybody. Sometimes I can be such an asshole."

"That's true. You're a nice asshole though."

"Thanks. Anyway, I'm sorry about giving you my opinions without your consent."

"It's alright. And for the record, I think you might be right about me. I may be going nuts."

"I never said nuts."

"Well, that's what you meant."

"OK, maybe I did. But there's nothing wrong with going nuts. It just means you're a human being in a fucked up world."

"I guess so."

"I'm always here for you, Nick, if you ever need to shoot the shit. Or the breeze. I'm versatile."

"Thanks."

"You wanna join me for breakfast?"

"Actually, I think I'm gonna go for a while. I need to figure some stuff out."

"Alright. Good luck." And his words came out soft and serious, as if he knows how unlucky I feel. Maybe he does.

Then I:

1. Pinch myself before I go, just in case.

2. Don't wake up.

I ring the doorbell and I'm afraid Cicely's going to:

1. Release her fury and grim passion.

2. Slap me.

3. Punish me.

Instead, she opens the door, and smiles. She says, "Hi hon."

Inside, I see an ant with a cybernetic thorax, serenading a piece of burnt toast in a kilt. And I see a Cyclops and an Eskimo on a trampoline tickling each other in mid air.

In other words:

1. Cicely hasn't stopped painting.

2. The world is right in the living room again.

It's my world that's wrong.

"I hope I didn't wake you," I say, because Cicely's wearing duck pirate pajamas.

"Well, I don't want to lie to you, hon," Cicely says, and scratches the top of her head with the tennis ball. "I was sleeping. On the plus side, I was just dreaming about talking to you, so thanks to you I get to live the dream. Except now you don't have spaghetti hair, and you're not wearing your birthday suit."

At this point, molten lava might be pumping through my face instead of blood. "I was naked?"

"No, it was just a special suit that you wear on your birthdays. It was made of turkey jerky. I thought that was a weird choice for a vegan, but I didn't say anything. Shall we sit?"

We sit.

And maybe I look as broken as I feel.

Because after a moment, Cicely says, "What happened?"

"Did I call you last night?" I say.

"No."

"Did I leave a message on your machine? You haven't checked yet. Could you check? If there's a message, please don't listen to it. Just erase it, OK?"

"OK," she says, soft.

"Could you check right now?"

"OK."

When she's gone, I:

    1. Bite my fingernails.

    2. Notice the origami animals hanging from the ceiling.

"There weren't any messages," Cicely says.

"Really?" I say, relieved.

"Really truly. What happened last night?"

"I don't know exactly. I can't remember."

"Are you OK?"

"Yeah."

"I shouldn't have asked that, because I know you're not OK. Either something really bad happened and you forgot to get dressed this morning, or you're here for an eleventh hour slumber party. Which is it?"

I:

    1. Look down at my boxers.

    2. Consider challenging her to a pillow fight.

    3. Say, "It's not important. I'd better go."

I don't want to, really. I want to tell her everything.

But maybe this curse isn't as simple as I thought.

Maybe people are given the power to look deep inside me and get a glimpse of:

    1. The things I've done.

    2. The secrets I've kept.

    3. The real me.

Maybe that's why they slap me.

And maybe this is the same old story about a person's past, and how there's nowhere left to hide.

If I can't keep my inner self in check anymore, I have to do what I can to protect Cicely from him.

Even if that means losing her forever.

Cicely takes my hand. "You can tell me, Nicholas. It's OK."

I can think of many other things to say, but still the words flood out of me.

"I called people last night. Friends and family. I don't remember any of it, but I know I said horrible things. I hurt them all deeply."

"How do you know what you said if you can't remember any of it?"

"I heard myself on my answering machine, talking to Gordon. I can't believe I talked to him that way."

"Then don't. Maybe it was someone else."

"No. It was me."

"How do you know that?"

"It was my voice. And I referred to a conversation that only Gordon and me knew about. Something's wrong with me, Cicely. I shouldn't be here."

Cicely squeezes my hand, soft. "It wasn't you. You're too kind."

"No I'm not," I almost say. Instead, I say nothing.

"Look, hon. We know the perpetrator behind our curses is capable of a wide array of dastardly deeds. He could have done this to you."

I want to believe her, but I know the man inside me too well. I'm afraid if I talk about him too much, I'll lose:

1. Myself again, like last night.

2. Cicely.

3. The last remnants of fairy tale feelings in my chest.

Still, to protect her, I say, "You don't know what I'm capable of."

"I don't care what you're capable of," Cicely says. "I care about how you choose to behave, and I don't think you would choose what happened last night."

"I wish I could believe that."

Cicely sighs. "You're breaking my heart, hon. You keep blaming yourself, but you're the one who was attacked." She points her finger at the creature in the swirling darkness on the wall. "He violated you, Nicholas."

I can feel his eyes on me, I think. "Maybe you're right."

"I'll prove it to you. You said you heard the message for Gordon on your answering machine?"

"Yeah."

"Does Gordon have a cell phone?"

"Yeah. I used his cell phone. I mean, the calls were made from his cell."

"Do you have a cell phone?"

"No."

Cicely smiles. "If you were the one who made the calls, why would you call Gordon using his own cell, instead of the house phone?"

"I don't know. Because I was drunk, and I decided to steal his phone, maybe."

"I think the perpetrator left a message on the machine, because he wanted you to hear it. He wanted you to doubt yourself. Do you usually listen to the messages first thing in the morning?"

"Yeah, if there are any."

"And you usually wake up before Gordon?"

"Yeah."

"Then there wasn't much of a chance Gordon would have listened to it first and deleted it. And let me guess. You found the cell phone in your room before Gordon took it back."

"How did you know that?"

"Because the perpetrator wanted you to see all the dialed numbers from last night. He thought of everything. Well, except me. I don't think he knows what I'm capable of."

My heart thrashes against my chest.

I thought I'd feel better if Cicely convinced me the enemy:

1. Isn't me.
2. Is, in fact, a psychopathic and intelligent bastard who can mimic voices, fuck with my life like no one else I've ever met, and possibly erase people from existence.

And maybe I do feel a little better.

But part of me wants to sleep:

1. Under the covers of my childhood bed.
2. Until the world is safe again.

In other words:

3. Forever.

Partway through *The City of Lost Children*, Cicely pauses the film and says, "Abby. You said none of your family friends wanted to join us for dinner?"

Abby nods.

I knew this confrontation would happen sooner or later, and I'm:

    1. Happy I'm here to see it.

    2. Jealous.

    3. Stupid.

    4. Pathetic.

"Did they give you any reason?" Cicely says.

Abby:

    1. Shakes her head.

    2. Looks a little pale.

"This is important," Cicely says. "I need to know exactly what they told you."

"I don't remember," Abby says.

"Let me guess then. They acted like you did something horrible."

Abby and me, our eyes widen. And Abby says, "I was afraid if I told you, you wouldn't like me anymore."

"Well, that's not going to happen, hon. You can tell us anything."

Abby picks at the eye of the stuffed ant on her lap. "They just said things like I should be ashamed for what I did. But I don't know what I did. My memories are all messed up, you know? What if I'm a bad person and I don't even know it?"

"You're not a bad person. The one who cursed us called all your friends and pretended to be you. The same thing happened to Nicholas."

Abby looks at me.

"It's true," I say, and I think I believe it.

"Why does he keep doing these things to us?" Abby says.

"I'll ask him when I see him," Cicely says, and there's more than a little fury twisting up her forehead.

Then I:

    1. Realize the obvious.

    2. Feel sick to my stomach.

"Cicely," I say. "If he's done this to Abby and me, you might be next."

This is probably the first time Cicely's considered this, judging by her:

1. Expression.
2. Silence.
3. Tendency to worry more about other people's problems than her own, I think.

Finally, she says, "Maybe he already did it. Not that I have many friends he could call. Well, aside from the imaginary unicorns living under my bed. But I don't think they can work phones." And even though she's talking like this, she's frowning. "He could've called John. My family. My parents." Her voice trembles. "Oh god."

"I'm sorry," Abby says.

And I say nothing, like an idiot.

"I haven't spoken to my parents for years," Cicely says. "If he broke that silence…god. I don't want to think about it."

Then Cicely:

1. Thinks about it, I'm sure.
2. Stares at the tennis ball.
3. Looks like she's fighting back tears.

There's no grim passion left in her eyes.

I realize Cicely:

1. Isn't a super hero.
2. Is a real human being, after all.

That means I need to be more than a sidekick who spends all day staring at his:

1. Mole.
2. Watch.
3. Pocket contents.

Just because I feel useless sometimes doesn't mean that I am.

I need to help her.

And right now, I:

1. Want to paint over the eyes on the wall that are staring at Cicely.
2. Can't help thinking about what Gordon told me about psychopaths, and how they get off on other people's suffering.

Then it hits me. Or it:

    1. Kicks me in the crotch.

Then:

    2. Smashes me over the head with a baseball bat.

"Cicely," I say. "You said before that you felt like someone was watching you, right?"

"Yes," Cicely says.

"I think you were right. I think he spies on us somehow. That's why our curses have lasting effects. He likes to watch us suffer. It also explains how the creature knew so much about me and Gordon when he left the message on the machine."

Cicely doesn't say, "You're crazy."

Instead, what she says is, "That makes sense."

And I say, "I'm guessing it wouldn't help us to search for hidden cameras or listening devices. He's probably using something non-mechanical. Something we can't detect. But we might want to look around for equipment just in case."

Abby:

    1. Holds the ant close to her chest.

    2. Glances around.

    3. Says, "Do you think he's watching right now?"

"I don't know," I say. "Maybe. Oh, and would you mind writing down the addresses of all the family friends you can remember?"

"Why?"

"I'd like to visit them. Ask them some questions. I might be able to tell if they're lying."

I don't tell them I used to be the Batman of Liars.

"Alright," Abby says. "I don't have the addresses memorized or anything, so I'll write them down for you when I get home."

"Thanks."

"Maybe there's something else we can do," Cicely says. "If you're right, and he feeds off our pain, maybe we can hide it from him."

"How?" Abby says.

"However we can."

So when I get home, I:

1. Delete the messages on my machine.
2. Think about my family.
3. Even think about Karl, who slapped me right outside the apartment and said, "I know you were lying about fucking Heather, but that was a low blow, man."

And then I cry:

1. Into my pillow.
2. In silence.
3. In the dark.

Because I'm not alone.

#26

IN MY DREAM, Cicely is Cicely. I'm trying to tell her how I won't let anyone rob her house, and she smiles.

I notice the window's boarded up. No one's watching us. Cicely tells me we can start singing if I stop growling so loud, but I'm not growling.

Then the creature crawls out of the hole in the floor. He's already eaten Gordon and Greg and I try to shield Cicely. But it's much too late to protect her.

Her face is already melting.

Outside of this nightmare, awake, I can't escape. In this room, I'm:

1. Naked.
2. Empty. And this emptiness reminds me of how I used to feel after drinking too much.
3. Alone.
4. Chained to a hook on the wall.

The growling from my dream now sounds more like a motor, but I can't see the source.

What I can see is:

1. A closed door.
2. A burlap bag on the cement floor.
3. A candle-lit table with a glass on top, filled with what looks like red wine.
4. An axe by my hand.

The deep rumbling stops, and for some reason I hold my breath.

Then I:

1. Grab the axe.

2. Hack at the chain.

3. Yank on the chain.

None of which does any good.

The door opens.

"Hiya, Nicky."

I expect the creature from my dream, almost.

Instead, he appears to be:

1. A white male.

2. Between the ages of 18 and 32.

And judging by his accent:

3. American.

And judging by his smirk and the fact that he's wearing my clothes:

4. An asshole.

"I hope you like this place," he says. "Because it's gonna be your home for the next two years." After a few moments of silence, he laughs. "No, I couldn't take care of a human. Too expensive. I'll let you go soon."

Sure, this situation is:

1. Fucked up.

But I can't help thinking it's also:

2. An opportunity to stop this guy, somehow.

I look at the axe, and wish I were Batman.

"Don't even think about it," the bastard says. "If you throw it, I'll just catch it and throw it at your face."

I throw the axe as hard as I can.

He doesn't:

1. Catch it.

2. Throw it at my face.

Instead, he dodges the blade, fast and easy.

"I didn't think you'd actually throw it, so I wasn't ready," he says. "I could've caught it though."

"Right," I say, crackle.

The asshole:

1. Grins.
2. Sits down on what looks like air.
3. Says, "It's all in the hamstrings. Now, you're probably wondering why I brought you here tonight."

At this point, I'm wondering what I should throw at this guy next, but I don't tell him that.

"Forget about stopping me for now," he says, as if he can read my mind. Maybe he can. "I need you to pay attention. Now, the reason you're here is because you seem a little confused about the nature of our relationship. And we're going to clear up that confusion right now." He yawns. "First of all, you should know that you can't hide your suffering from me. That's just…stupid. Even if I couldn't see or hear your pain, I could still taste it, smell it, feel it in my gut. There's no point trying to defy me or stop me. I'll always end up on top." Then he stands, and steps closer to me. "To instill this truth in you, I decided to kidnap, or dognap I should say, Gordon's little bitch. She's in that bag there. Go ahead and check if you want."

I:

1. Don't want to check at all.
2. Look inside the bag.

She's there. Her eyes are open, and she:

1. Doesn't look at me.
2. Could be dead.

A bitter rage gushes from my stomach to my head, like acid reflux.

"I filled her with fear," the asshole says. "So she won't be able to move for a while. She's completely at your mercy."

I glare at him.

"I was going to let you use the axe," the bastard says. "But since you threw it at me, you lost your axe privileges. Now you have to stomp her to death."

"Fuck you," I growl.

"No, Nicky. You're fucked. The dog's fucked. Not me."

"If you hurt her, I'll kill you."

He chuckles. "Didn't you hear what I said? You're the one who's going to kill her. Although now that I think about it, stomping her might not be the best idea without any shoes on. Maybe you could strangle her."

I yank on the chain again.

He takes another step forward and says, "Remember the McDonald Triad Gordon told you about? I'm thinking you could try out the whole triangle and let me know how you like it. First you kill her, then you drench her with gasoline and light her on fire. Finally, you piss all over her. That's not exactly bedwetting, I know, but it's close enough." He laughs again.

I want to:

    1. Break free.

    2. Wrap the chain around his neck like he's Jabba the Hutt.

"I'm just kidding," he says. "You only need to kill her."

"I would never hurt Meta," I say.

"If you don't, I'll make you eat your own foot. No, that's not my style at all. That's sick." He takes another step.

And I spring forward.

At the last moment, he backs away and avoids my curled fingers by a few inches.

"One of my favorite shows is gonna be on soon," he says. "I don't have a VCR or TiVo, so let's hurry this up, OK?"

I glance over at the wine glass.

"I wouldn't throw that," the asshole says. "You're gonna need that if you want to get out of here alive. But before we get to that step, you need to kill the fucking dog."

I:

    1. Don't move.

    2. Attack him with my eyes.

"You're not helping yourself by resisting me," he says. "Defiance just makes it that much more satisfying when I get what I want. And I will."

I can't think of anything else to say but, "No."

He laughs. "You don't understand, Nicky. I always get what I want. That's no exaggeration."

"I don't care. I'd rather die than hurt Meta."

"I'm afraid that's not one of your options. Either you do what I say, or I'm gonna do something a lot worse. Worse than a dead dog or even a melting face. It's pretty much the worst thing I can think of, and I've had a long time to think."

"You're wasting your time."

"Really? So you don't mind if I do this worst thing to someone you know?"

I imagine this bastard:

1. Placing his hand on Sol's sweating forehead.
2. Forcing the most intense pain possible inside Sol's body, as he shakes all over.

Then I imagine myself:

1. Wrapping my hands around Meta's soft throat.
2. Squeezing as hard as I can, as she gazes in my eyes.

I can almost hear:

1. My dad screaming.
2. Meta whimpering.

I turn around to hide my tears.

"You know, you were wrong about me," the asshole says. "I don't always need to witness your suffering to enjoy myself. Sometimes just knowing what you're going through is enough to make me warm and fuzzy."

I face him again and say, "If that's true, why don't you leave and let me suffer alone?"

"No, you don't know all the rules yet. Plus, you might need someone to help you get through this. Killing a beloved pet isn't easy, I know. But honestly, you should be thankful I didn't decide to bring Svetlana in that bag."

"Stay away from her."

He flicks his hand at me. "I know, I know. You're not ready for someone like her yet. We'll focus on the dog for now."

I:

1. Rush to the table.
2. Grab the glass.
3. Don't care if he dodges it.

Right now I just want to break something like a child.

"Hold on," the fucking bastard says. "That's your ticket out of here. I already told you that."

Maybe if I throw the glass near his feet, he'll end up stepping on the shards.

"Drink the wine," he says. "And I'll set you free. I'll even take the fear out of the dog. Then, for the rest of the night, I'll let you attack me with everything you've got. I promise I won't fight back either."

"There's no way I'm gonna trust you," I say.

"I understand your feelings, but what else are you gonna do? If you don't drink the wine, I'll leave you and the dog down here to die of thirst. Although Meta will probably have a heart attack before it ever comes to that. I know you're scared, but you couldn't imagine what she's feeling right now. I'm sure she'd ask you to kill her if she could."

"The fuck she would."

"I'm not trying to insinuate anything negative about her character, Nicky. I'm saying any living thing, myself included, would rather die than feel what she's feeling. Fear can be worse than pain sometimes."

I stare at the:

1. Burlap bag.
2. Wine glass.

"You want to stop Meta's suffering," he says. "So why are you hesitating?"

"I don't want to die," I say, more to myself.

"The wine won't kill you," he says. "Part of you must know how much I value your life. I wouldn't have put so much energy into you otherwise."

I eye the bastard again. "If that's true, then you won't let me die of thirst, even if I don't drink this. Give me my clothes and let us go."

"First of all, these aren't your clothes. I made these myself, so that they'd look like your clothes. Your clothes are actually back in your apartment. Second, I do value your life, but only as long as you're living on my terms. So I'm giving you an opportunity to survive. If you'd rather die than drink my wine, it sounds like you're the one who's not cherishing the gift of life."

I:

1. Look into the glass.

2. Haven't let alcohol inside me for years.

But I:

3. Can't think of any alternatives.

4. Want free of this chain, now.

The asshole grins.

Suddenly, all my doubts scream inside me again, and I know I:

1. Shouldn't trust this monster.

2. Have to find another way.

But I already drank the wine.

And I don't attempt to:

1. Rescue Meta.

2. Fight the psychopath.

3. Bring him down.

Because it's much too late for any of that.

I'm already collapsing.

Awake, I find myself:

1. In my room.

2. Sweating.

3. Wearing the same clothes I fell asleep in last night.

I scramble out the door.

In the living room, Meta's resting on her favorite chair.

Alive.

"Are you alright?" I say.

She hops off the chair and licks my feet.

I:

1. Kneel down in front of her.

2. Wrap my arms around her.

And as everything that happened to me last night swirls inside me, I:

3. Cry into her fur.

She doesn't move away.

"I'm sorry," I say, meaning I'm:

    1. Not only sorry about her suffering.

    2. Apologizing for thinking about choking her.

"I'm so sorry."

"Morning," Gordon says, behind me. "Well, afternoon."

I turn around. "Are you alright?

"For the most part." He heads for the couch.

"Why? Did something happen?"

"Just woke up with a fuck of a headache."

"Oh."

"Are you crying?"

"No," I almost say. But the thought of lying makes me sick to my stomach. So instead, I say, "Yeah."

"Do you want to talk about it?"

"Yeah, but if I told you what happened, you'd say I'm crazy or that I was dreaming." My voice cracks. "I can't deal with that right now. I gotta go. I hope you feel better soon."

"Thanks."

Then I go to my room, because the psychopath threatened to do something worse than horrible to someone I know, if I didn't kill Meta.

In other words, someone on my speed dial might already be:

    1. Violated.

    2. Broken.

    3. Gone.

So I call:

    1. Karl.

"Are you alright?" I say, and I feel guilty because part of me's hoping he's the one the psychopath chose.

"Like you even give a shit," Karl says.

"I do."

"Right."

"Why else would I be calling you?"

"Man, because you love fucking with people's lives. You always have. You've never given a shit about anyone."

"That's not true."

"Why'd you tell me you fucked Heather then?"

"I never slept with Heather."

"I know you didn't. I'm just saying you like ruining my life."

"I've never ruined your life."

"I was a good kid before I met you, man. I'd never even sipped a beer. Or did you forget that?"

"I never forced you to drink with me."

"Maybe you didn't put a gun to my head. But if me and you never met back then, things would be better for me. Heather would still be here right now. So fuck you, Nick. I'm not gonna let you kick me while I'm down anymore."

I take a deep breath, and decide to lie, no matter how it makes me feel. "I had a nightmare last night, where something terrible happened to you. It felt so real, I just want to make sure you're OK."

Karl's silent for a while. "I'm sorry I've been such an asshole. I don't know what's wrong with me. You've always been a good friend."

"No, I haven't."

He laughs. "You're right."

"I know I've said this to you before, but I'm sorry about how I treated you when we were roommates."

"When did you ever apologize to me before?"

"Years ago."

"I don't remember that."

"Well, it's a good thing I said it again then."

"Yeah."

"So you're alright?"

"I'm fine. Nothing a good fuck couldn't fix, right?"

"I'll talk to you later."

 2. Nadia.

"Are you alright?" I say.

"Of course not," Nadia says.

"What happened?"

"Don't play dumb with me, Nicky. Greg told me that he called you. You know what you did."

"It wasn't me."

"Maybe you can't remember because you were too drunk. But it doesn't matter. I remember. I'll always remember what you said."

"Nadia, I'm calling because I had a nightmare last night. About you and Greg and Svetlana. I just want to make sure—"

"I can't talk with you when you're like this, Nicky. When I do, I feel so angry. I feel…hatred."

Her words sink deep inside me. I feel dizzy.

"But, I mean…I don't really hate you," she says. "I hate the enemy inside you."

I don't tell her, "The only enemy in here is me."

Instead, I stare at my mole.

She says, "As much as I want to save you, I can't. I can't treat you with the love that you deserve. You need God for that. Without God, you'll always fail everyone. Me, you, everyone."

"I wasn't the one who called you."

"I…can't be your sister anymore," she says. "I mean…I'll always be your sister by blood. But until you become a better man, I can't be anything more than that."

Tears trickle down my face, and I can't think of anything else to say but, "Nadia."

"It's for the best, Nicky." She sounds like she's crying too. "Goodbye."

"Nadia."

She hangs up.

   3. Sol.

"Are you alright?" I say, and I hold my breath.

"I'm worried about you, Nicholas. Brienda and I are both very worried. I hope you've called to tell me that you're getting help for yourself."

"I haven't started drinking again, Sol."

"If that's true, then you left that terrible message our machine without any alcohol in your body. That's almost worse. No matter what's happening with you, son, you need help."

"I know this sounds crazy, but I wasn't the one who left the message. It was someone else."

"I know it must feel that way."

"I'm telling the truth, Dad."

"I wish I could believe that."

"You can."

"I love you, son, and I'll always be here for you. But I need you to be honest with me. You can tell me what's really bothering you. You don't have to make up problems."

"This is real."

Sol doesn't speak for a few heartbeats. "Is this about your mother?"

"No."

"Are you having nightmares again?"

"Not about her."

"Maybe we could talk about our memories of her. Brienda thinks that might help."

"I need to go, Dad. I have an appointment."

"OK. I love you, son."

"I love you too, Dad."

"Do you need me to come over?"

"No, Dad. I'm fine."

4. Cicely.

I know it can't be her. She's too strong. She's Cicely.

Still, I cringe after every ring, and my imagination swells with horror.

I see her chained to a wall.

Then she's trapped in the burlap sack.

She's screaming, thrashing, begging.

By the time the answering machine picks up, I'm shaking.

"Cicely?" I say. "Are you there?" Then I realize I need to wait until after the beep, so I do. "Are you there, Cicely? It's me. It's Nicholas. I need you. I need to talk to you. Are you home?"

"Hi hon," Cicely says.

I grin, and feel guilty, because someone I know could be suffering. "Are you alright?"

"Well, I was ambushed this morning—"

"What happened?"

"I was ambushed by a horde of robotic radishes. I managed to scramble their circuits by using my refrigerator magnets like ninja stars, but I'm still not positive who sent them after me. I'm thinking it was either Robby the Robot or Carmen Sandiego, although I've heard rumors that Carmen converted to Luddism after a recent run-in with the Brave Little Toaster's evil twin. So she might not associate with those of the robotic persuasion anymore. Plus, she hates radishes. Or is it parsnips? Anyway, besides all of that, I'm peachy. I even smell like peaches, thanks to my new soap."

"So nothing happened last night? This morning?"

"No." Her voice sounds soft and serious now. "What happened?"

I still haven't decided how much I want to tell her. She's dealing with so much already. But more importantly, I want to be close to her when I relive last night.

"I'll tell you when I come over," I say. "Is it alright if I come over?"

"Of course," she says. "Anytime, hon."

"Thanks. Oh." I feel guilty again, because I didn't think of this sooner. "Have you talked to Abby today?"

"Not yet."

"I'd better call her."

"Nicholas...did he hurt you?"

"I'm afraid he hurt someone else. You're sure you're alright?"

"I'm sure. Come over soon, OK?"

"OK." And I don't know how this could possibly help, but still, I say, "Be careful."

5. Abby.

"Are you alright?" I say.

I don't hear anything for so long, I'm afraid we've been disconnected. Then she says, "Leave my friends alone."

"What?"

"You already took everything else from me. Isn't that enough?"

"Abby, it's me."

"I'm not as stupid as you think, you know. The real Nick doesn't have my phone number."

"I wrote it down in my purple notebook. Remember?"

She's silent for a while. "You're right. Sorry. But how do I know it's really you?"

"I guess because I'm calling to ask if you're alright. I don't think he'd have any reason to do that."

"That's true."

"Are you alright?"

"Yeah."

"How's the stab wound?"

"It's good. How are you?"

"I've been better."

"I'm sorry."

"Thanks."

"I know you're probably not the monster, Nick, but if you are, this might be my only chance to talk to you. I just want to know if my family's alive somewhere."

"I'm not him, Abby."

"OK. Do you think they're alive?"

I can't find enough hope inside me to say, "Of course."

So instead, I say, "I don't know."

"How do you deal with it?" she says. "I mean, not knowing what happened to your mom."

"It'd probably be better to talk with someone else about this. I'd better go."

"I'll give you the addresses when we meet up at Cicely's."

"Addresses?"

"You know. For the family friends. You asked me yesterday."

"Oh yeah. Thanks."

"Nick, do you think we could hang out sometime?"

"We're both going to Cicely's, right?"

"Yeah. But I mean a one-on-one sort of thing. You and Cicely are such good friends and everything. I usually don't get much chance to talk with you when we're all together."

"Oh."

"So, can we hang out sometime?"

I grimace at the idea, but she lost her family. And I stabbed her. "Alright."

"Great! Where do you want to go?"

"Anywhere's fine."

"I really hope you're not the monster."

"I'm not."

After hanging up, I:

1. Put down the phone.
2. Wipe my sweaty palm on my pants.
3. Consider that the psychopath only threatened to hurt someone I know in order to scare me.
4. Hope everyone's alive and well.
5. Return to the living room.
6. Sit beside Meta.

"I really fucked up," Gordon says.

"What happened?" I say.

Gordon grabs his hair with both hands. "I had an epiphany while you were in your room. And not the good kind where you realize life is beautiful or you want to become a rock star. This is one of those moments of clarity where you finally see yourself for the monster you are."

"You're not a monster."

"OK, I'm a dick then. Here you are, all traumatized by whatever happened to you last night, and you're too afraid to talk to me. Because I've given you every reason to be. I'm an asshole."

"You're a good guy."

"I read about this poll recently, taken by Amnesty International a few years back. Out of I think 1000 people, over a quarter thought if a woman gets raped and she's wearing revealing clothing at the time, she's either partially or fully responsible. After reading that, I wanted to scream at all those fuckers for blaming the victim. Then what do I do after you tell me some psychopath may be after you? I blame you. Jesus fuck, I'm the king of hypocrisy."

"You were just trying to help me."

"Don't defend my behavior, Nick. It's not gonna do either of us any good."

"Sorry."

"The most fucked up part of all this is that I've been denying your experiences the same way other assholes have denied mine. I've talked to a fuckload of family and friends about the sort of hatred that's directed at me because I'm disabled, but most people don't take me seriously. They think I'm lying or exaggerating. Maybe the truth just doesn't mesh with their view of reality, and they don't want to believe I could be treated so unfairly for no good reason. Maybe that's why I didn't want to believe you. But you deserve better than that. You've treated me with more respect than anyone else in my whole fucking life. So if you want to talk to me about what happened to you, I'll listen. With open ears and an open mind. No pressure though. I'd understand if I'm the last person you'd want to open up to."

He's not.

In fact, he's almost the first:

> 1. Cicely.
>
> 2. Sol.
>
> 3. Gordon.

"I'll tell you everything," I say. "But first, I really need to go to the bathroom."

"Thanks."

"For having to pee?"

"Shut up, Nick."

Inside the bathroom, I find:

> 1. A collage of photographs on the wall, all of a woman in her house, her yard, her car. In each photograph, I only see a part of her body. A hand, a leg, but never her face.

2. A letter taped to the mirror, in my handwriting.

3. Blood in the sink.

I remove the letter from the mirror, slow and careful, and read:

Dear Nicky,

I told you I always get what I want, and that's true. The only reason you didn't kill Meta like I asked you to is because I didn't want you to kill her. I only wanted to inspire you to choose a dog's life over a human's. So now you're responsible for what I'm about to do. Of course, by the time you read this letter, the deed will already be done, and I'll be at home watching my stories.

By the way, that's not really blood in the sink. It's water and food coloring. Also, I wanted to mention that I borrowed some of your old lists a while back so I could learn your handwriting. I hope you don't mind.

Anyway, have a great day.

Sincerely,

Pete, your friendly neighborhood overlord.

P.S. I've written down Ruth's address on the back of this letter. You might want to pay her a visit.

P.P.S. You think you don't know anyone named Ruth? Think again.

I don't know anyone named Ruth, but I:

1. Find the directions to the address online.

2. Drive there with the urge to drive faster, but I'm not Batman, and I could hurt someone.

3. Recognize the house from the photographs in my bathroom.

My heart thumps, hard.

I try to restrain myself, but my imagination swells with hope.

I see my mother answering the door.

Then she hugs me tight.

She's beaming, crying, explaining.

My mother's name wasn't Ruth when I knew her, but things change.

I knock, soft.

And the door opens.

"Kin," I say.

"Can I help you?" Kin says.

"I wanted to know if you're alright."

She crosses her arms. "Is this some religious thing?"

"What do you mean?"

"Whatever god you're ballyhooing, I'm not interested."

"I'm not trying to ballyhoo anything, Kin. I just had a nightmare last night, and you were hurt. I want to make sure you're OK."

"What kind of sick tactic is this? Are you supposed to be my knight in shining armor?"

"It's not like that. I care about you, Kin."

"Would you stop calling me that? I have family, and you're not one of them."

A terrible thought claws its way inside me. "Ruth?"

"How do you know my name?"

"I'm Abby's friend."

"I don't know any Abby. Whatever list I'm on, take me off it. I don't want you or any of your people bothering me here again."

"This is gonna sound crazy, but we know each other. Someone made you forget me. I think he made you forget yourself too. Your name is Kin."

"I don't believe in past lives or whatever you're getting at. Does this nonsense ever work on anyone?"

"I'm only trying to help."

"Your time would be better spent with someone off-center and gullible. I'd suggest the neighbors."

"I'm telling the truth."

"Your truth isn't my truth, kid." She sighs. "I'm starting to feel a little sorry for you, so I'm going to leave you with a little advice. You don't need anyone else to agree with you for your beliefs to be important. As soon as you accept that, your life will be a whole lot less frustrating. Now go home and think about that for a while." She takes a step back.

Then I:

1. Take a step forward.
2. Say, "Kin, wait."
3. Receive #26 on my right cheek.

She looks at me with those I-don't-know-what-got-into-me eyes. And I want to tell her exactly who he is.

Instead, I say, "I'm sorry."

She:

1. Opens her mouth like she's going to speak.
2. Sighs.
3. Closes the door.

I want to:

1. Knock hard until she answers.
2. Tell her I had the chance to save her.
3. Apologize for failing.

But I don't.

When I return to my car, I find a letter on my windshield.

I read:

Dear Nicky,

In case you're not clear about what happened, Kin's gone. I removed her from existence and I replaced her with Ruth, who I created in my spare time on Saturday.

You probably think I did all this to hurt you, but that's only half the truth.

I wanted you to learn a little something about what I'm capable of.

Your fiend,

   Pete.

P.S. We only come into contact if and when I desire it. If you and your friends don't stop looking for me, I'm going to do the same thing to Cicely that I did to Kin.

P.P.S. Wash your car. It's filthy.

Standing by the front door, I decide not to tell Cicely about:

   1. Kin's removal from reality.

   2. My kidnapping.

   3. The letters.

Telling her all this would only make her want to find the psychopath that much more.

And I'd do anything to keep Cicely away from him, even if it means:

   1. Lying to her.

   2. Sabotaging all her efforts.

I stand there a few more minutes before ringing the doorbell.

Then Cicely hugs me, tight. "How are you, hon?"

I say, crackle, "I'm fine."

"Shall we move to the couch?"

We move.

Cicely holds my hand. "Is everyone OK?"

"What do you mean?" I say.

"On the phone you said the perpetrator may have hurt someone. Did you find out anything?"

"Everyone's fine. I just had a nightmare last night. It seemed so real, and I overreacted. I'm sorry."

"Don't worry about it, hon."

I feel like:

>   1. Crying.

>   2. Throwing up.

>   3. Rolling myself up in the pastel blanket beside me.

But I manage to:

>   1. Sit there.

>   2. Smile a little.

>   3. Say, "Do you have any new leads?"

And Cicely says, "A little bird told me she knew the whereabouts of our perpetrator, but it turned out she was only trying to con me out of my worm farm. So I ate her for lunch. Other than that, nothing to report."

Cicely and me, we watch *Happiness of the Katakuris* until Abby shows up.

"Would you like some snowflake sweat?" Cicely says.

"That means water, right?" Abby says.

"Right."

"That'd be good."

Cicely heads into the kitchen.

"Did you call me earlier?" Abby says, sitting on the chair beside me.

"Yeah," I say.

"Thank goodness."

Cicely returns with the water.

"Why don't you take my seat?" I say. "You've got a stab wound, and the couch is more comfortable."

But the real reason I want to move is because it's painful to sit so close to Cicely.

"Thanks," Abby says.

Then I:

>   1. Get up.

>   2. Walk toward Abby to help her up.

>   3. Trip on my shoelace.

>   4. Fall.

My:

    1. Hand springs forward at her face.

    2. Elbow knocks over her glass of water.

    3. Knee lands hard on her right foot.

And Abby:

    1. Yells.

    2. Grabs her face.

    3. Recoils her legs.

"I'm so sorry," I say.

"Don't worry about it," Abby says, lowering her hands.

"I'll be right back," Cicely says.

"Did I break anything?" I say. "How's your foot?"

"I'm alright," Abby says, as blood oozes from her forehead.

"I'm really sorry, Abby. I should be more careful."

"It was just an accident."

Cicely comes back and:

    1. Wipes away the blood under the cut with a washcloth.

    2. Says, "Can I apply some clay?"

"Is that your nickname for antibiotics?" Abby says.

"No, it's Terramin clay. It'll help."

"Alright."

While Cicely dabs the clay on her forehead, Abby:

    1. Smiles at me.

    2. Says, "At least you weren't holding a knife this time."

I don't:

    1. Laugh.

    2. Smile back.

    3. Feel any better.

Maybe I convinced myself that my curse brought about the stabbing so that she would slap me.

But there was no slap this time.

And I know these accidents have:

    1. Nothing to do with my curse.

    2. Everything to do with the fact that I'm not cut out to connect with anyone.

"All done," Cicely says. "Take two mermaid scales and call me in the morning."

"Thanks," Abby says. Then she offers me a piece of paper. "It's all the addresses you wanted."

"Oh," I say. "Thanks. I'll check them out tomorrow."

"Do you want me to come with you?" Cicely says.

"No, I'll be alright," I say, fast. "It's easier for me to catch someone in a lie if I set up the traps myself."

"OK."

"So Nick," Abby says. "When do you want to go out?"

And I:

    1. Stare at my knees.

    2. Say, "Anytime."

"What about tonight?" Abby says.

"Not tonight," I say. "I have a lot of work to do. I should go, actually."

I don't want to, really. But what I want doesn't matter anymore.

Back inside my car, I hold the paper Abby gave me, and I know there's a slight chance the addresses might lead to Pete.

So I not only rip apart:

    1. The paper.

But:

    2. Something precious inside me.

Because from now on, I have to:

    1. Suffer alone.

    2. Let loose the deceitful asshole I used to be.

I need a drink.

And of course, feeling this way is a warning sign. I know I'm on road to hurting:

    1. Myself.

    2. Everyone around me.

But in the end, I'd rather live in my own hell than the one Pete would create for me.

Something taps my window and I:

    1. Tighten up all over.

    2. Expect to see Pete standing there, holding a burlap bag, smirking at me.

Instead, I see Cicely.

After I roll down the window, she says, "Can I come in?"

I nod.

Then she:

    1. Joins me in the car.

    2. Says, "What happened to you last night, Nicholas?"

"Nothing," I say.

"You don't have to go through this alone."

"Nothing happened, Cicely."

"Then why is every fiber of my being telling me a different story?"

"Because you're imagining things."

Cicely:

    1. Sighs.

    2. Draws a horned duck on the window with her finger.

I glance at my watch.

She faces me again and the sight of her tears rolling down her face makes my chest hurt.

"Please tell me," she says, crackles.

"I can't," I say.

"Why?"

"Because you'll disappear from me."

Then she:

    1. Wipes her tears with the tennis ball.

    2. Sniffles.

    3. Holds my hand.

    4. Says, "I'm not going anywhere."

Love and hatred swirl around inside me.

Love toward Cicely.

And hatred towards the way I've been acting.

Cicely deserves:

    1. Honesty.

    2. Respect.

And maybe Cicely's so sad because she can't be friends with another John. She won't.

But even after all my lies, she's giving me another chance.

"He'll kill you if you try to find him," I say. "He told me. Please don't look for him anymore."

"I won't," she says, soft.

"You won't?"

"I don't want to die, hon. I want to stop this guy so that we can live happier lives. If looking for him would only make things worse, then I'll find another way."

"What if there is no other way?"

"Then I'll give up." She squeezes my hand. "Do you want to tell me more about what happened?"

I tell her more.

In fact, I tell her everything.

#27

IN MY DREAM, my mother's back. I'm trying to tell her how sorry I am that I forgot her birthday, but she can't hear me. Or maybe she's ignoring me.

I notice a man outside the window. He's watching us. He's ugly, with urine gushing out his nostrils, but he's still Pete. I draw the curtains.

Then my mother's body contorts. Her head spins and her knees smash together so hard and red sparks swarm at me.

So I push her toward the hole in the floor, where she'll fall deep down in the darkness.

She tells me her reasons to live.

But I don't care enough to stop.

Outside of this nightmare, awake, I escape to my workstation.

And I try to think of the perfect plush to make for Cicely.

I come up with a:

1. Yard gnome.

2. Spork.

3. Pastel Godzilla.

In other words, I fail.

After Gordon wakes up, I join him in the kitchen.

"I'm sorry I ran off yesterday," I say. "I really did want to talk to you. I would've talked to you last night, but you were already asleep when I got back."

"No worries," Gordon says. "Did your crisis end up alright?"

"No. The psychopath went after a woman I know. He killed her."

"Oh shit. I'm sorry, Nick. Did you already call the police?"

"They wouldn't believe me. Kin didn't really die in a way they'd recognize."

"Jesus fuck, what does that mean?"

"Her body's still alive. But he destroyed everything else. He made her into someone else."

Gordon taps his finger on the table. "Maybe it would help if you started from the beginning."

So I do.

And Gordon:

1. Listens.

2. Rubs his chin.

3. Cries.

Afterward, he says, "I'm sorry he hurt you."

"Thanks," I say.

"I'm gonna help you however I can."

"It'd help me the most if you moved."

"Yeah, well, that's not gonna happen."

"He could hurt you, Gordon. And if that happened, it'd be my fault."

"No, it'd be Pete's fault."

"But I'm the one who got you involved."

"I'm involved because a psychopath is fucking with my best friend. Not to mention what he did to Meta."

"He could kill you."

"Now, are you treating me like an overbearing parent because I'm your friend or because I'm blind? Nevermind, you don't have to answer that. Whatever the reason is, it doesn't justify you treating me this way."

"I'm sorry."

"Thanks. Don't get me wrong, Nick. I'm glad you care about me and all, but you're not my protector, and you don't need to blame yourself if I get hurt. I'm capable of making my own decisions."

"You're right. I'm sorry."

"Don't sweat it." He stands. "Can I hug you?"

"Yeah," I say.

We hug.

And Gordon's more than my friend right now, even if he doesn't know it. He's another reason to live.

I think about:

    1. Gordon's expertise in all things psychopathic.

    2. The many times he helped me when I was sure no one could.

And for a few fleeting moments:

    1. The world is right in the apartment again.

    2. I feel safe.

The note on the door tells me that:

    1. My new nickname is Nickknack.

    2. I'm welcome to wait inside.

    3. I might want to hurry, because Cicely spotted a flock of hungry-looking flying monkeys on the roof earlier.

Inside, I see a grass hut with chicken legs, tightroping a genie's extra-long ear hair over a fondue volcano. And I don't see what else is new, because as the creature in the swirling darkness invades my vision:

    1. My eyes freeze.

    2. Fear trickles down my back.

Cicely could be out there right now, dooming herself in an effort to find Pete.

"She's fine," I say, and most of me believes it.

The horror dissipates.

I trust her.

For a few minutes I work on the pattern for a fire hydrant plush I need to create, but then Cicely and Abby come in.

"What happened?" I say, because Abby's crying.

"She wanted to visit Kin," Cicely says.

"Oh."

Abby sits beside me on the couch, close.

I glance at my watch.

"You were right, Nick," Abby says, wiping her tears. "She's gone. She didn't remember me at all."

"I'm sorry," I say.

"We have to do what he says, or he'll kill us too."

"We won't let that happen," Cicely says.

Abby:

    1. Jiggles her knee up and down.

    2. Bites at her fingernail.

"My alien parasite is starving," Cicely says. "Shall we eat?"

We eat.

Although Abby hardly touches her food.

"I was thinking," Cicely says, tapping her tennis ball on the table. "Maybe we could hire a sketch artist and get ourselves a drawing of Pete."

"But," I say, fast. "You said you weren't gonna look for him anymore."

"And I won't. I think it might be safer for us if we can recognize him. If we see him somewhere, we'll know to run the other way."

Then I:

    1. Look into her eyes.

    2. Nod.

    3. Say, "We don't need a sketch artist."

    4. Draw Pete's smirking face in my purple notebook.

Cicely and Abby study the page.

I wait for a look of recognition to invade their faces, because this asshole might be someone they know.

But they only stare.

"Thank you," Cicely says.

"Can I stay here tonight?" Abby says.

"Of course, hon," Cicely says. "Anytime."

And once again, the surge of jealousy in my chest reminds me that I'm:

    1. Stupid.

    2. Pathetic.

    3. The same asshole I always was.

Later, the three of us head into the living room to see one of Cicely's favorite films, *The Lost Skeleton of Cadavra.*

Before we sit, Abby:

    1. Says, "Oh yeah. I want to show you something."

    2. Fishes a piece of paper from her pocket.

And I:

    1. Approach her.

    2. Stumble.

    3. Fall forward.

    4. Grab at her.

    5. Feel the sting as she slaps me.

    6. Say, "Fuck, I'm sorry. Are you alright?"

"Yeah," she says. "I'm sorry, Nick. I didn't mean to do that."

"I know. Are you bleeding?"

"No. You barely touched it."

Of course she's:

    1. Referring to her stab wound.

    2. Lying.

I watch Cicely help Abby to the couch, then I:

    1. Turn around.

    2. Look at the spot of the rug where I tripped.

There's nothing there.

"I'd better go," I say.

"It was an accident," Cicely says. "It was the curse."

Or maybe part of me is hurting her on purpose.

And maybe deep down, in the darkness of my heart, I don't care enough to stop.

Eventually, Abby:

    1. Shows me the flyer for a new insect exhibit at the museum.

    2. Says, "You wanna go?"

And after everything I've done to her, I don't know how to say no.

So I don't.

Abby and me, we watch the giant animatronic grasshopper:

1. Open and close its mandibles.

2. Move its antennae.

"Have you ever heard of a hairworm?" Abby says.

"I don't think so," I say.

"It's this parasite that lives inside grasshoppers. When the hairworm's old enough, it messes with the grasshopper's central nervous system. You know what happens next?"

"No."

"The hairworm forces the grasshopper to commit suicide by jumping into water. In the water, the hairworm can swim off and find a mate. Isn't that weird?"

"Definitely weird."

And with this scenario in mind, I can't help but think of Pete and his manipulations.

Then again, this comparison is an insult to parasites everywhere.

Pete's not surviving.

He's violating.

"Lots of people wonder about beached whales," Abby says. "Why they do it, you know? I think it's probably some sort of parasite like the hairworm that needs to get on land."

"That's interesting," I say.

"I hope they have a big robot ant in one of the rooms."

"That'd be nice."

"Did you know some birds put ants on their bodies or rub them on their feathers?"

"I didn't know that."

"It's called anting. There are lots of reasons they might do it, but some people think they use the formic acid from the ants to kill mites and fungi and stuff. Oh, and rooks even fumigate their wings with cigarette smoke. People say bird brain like it's a bad thing, but birds are really smart."

"Yeah."

"I still like ants the best though."

"Why is that?"

"I don't know. I can't remember." Her beaming face wilts fast.

"You know, maybe the fact that you like ants says something about your family."

"What do you mean?"

"Well, ants live in close-knit groups, and they get along well. Maybe you connect with that because your family was the same way."

Then Abby:

1. Says, "Maybe."

2. Looks down at her feet.

3. Cries.

Obviously, it was stupid of me to think I could offer her more than:

1. Injuries.

2. Pain.

"I'm sorry," I say.

Abby:

1. Wipes her eyes.

2. Sniffles.

3. Says, "I need to tell you something."

"Alright," I say.

"Not here with all these people."

So we speed through the rest of the exhibit. And Abby never slows down, even when we pass the massive worker ant.

Inside the car, Abby:

1. Locks her door.

2. Looks into my eyes.

3. Starts crying again.

I think about:

1. Holding her hand.

2. Telling her that I'm here for her.

But instead, I study my mole.

"I did something terrible," Abby says. "I'm afraid you'll hate me if I tell you."

"I won't hate you," I say.

"How do you know that?"

"I just know. You can tell me."

She:

    1. Picks at a scab on her knee.

    2. Says, "Yesterday, I thought about…killing you."

And I:

    1. Bite at my fingernail.

    2. Say, "Because…I keep hurting you?"

"No!" she says. "What kind of person do you think I am?"

"Sorry."

"I've never wanted to hurt you or anything. It's just that Pete left me this note. He said if I killed you, he'd give me my life back. My family and my memories and everything. He said all I have to do is say this one special word. Then you'd die instantly, without any pain at all. And a few times…I thought about saying it."

New tears spill down her face, and I look away. "It's alright, Abby. I understand."

"I don't want you to be afraid of me. I'll never say the word. I promise."

"I believe you."

"The word isn't a normal one. So you don't have to worry about me saying it on accident either."

"That's good to know."

"Even if Pete really did give me back everything he took from me, I'd never be happy with you gone. My whole life would be about regretting what I did to you." She rubs her eyes with her palms. "I care about you a lot, Nick."

And I think about telling her:

    1. She's better off saying the special word.

    2. I'll only end up causing her more pain.

    3. Part of me deserves to be sacrificed.

But instead, I say, "Thanks."

"There's something else I gotta tell you," she says. "It's not as bad as the last thing, but it's still bad."

"Alright."

"I know how terrible you feel for stabbing me and hurting me. But it's not your fault at all, Nick. I let you suffer and blame yourself because I didn't want to tell you the truth."

I stare at her face. "What is the truth?"

"My curse isn't just about me losing my family. Pete made it so that things hurt me."

"What sort of things?"

"Everything. I get into accidents all the time, but they're not really accidents. The whole world is against me. And the only reason you hurt me more often than other things is because you need to get slapped every day. So our curses are sort of attracted to each other, you know? They fit together."

"Why didn't you tell me this before?"

"I'm dangerous, and I thought you wouldn't want to be around me anymore." She continues picking at her scab. "I'm really sorry, Nick. I'll stay away from you guys if you want me to."

Then she:

1. Takes a deep breath.
2. Looks me in the eyes, as if I have the power to decide her fate. Maybe I do.

"We're in this together," I say, holding her hand.

She beams, bright.

And for a few fleeting moments, so do I.

Maybe part of me is still:

1. Stupid.
2. Pathetic.
3. The same asshole I always was.

But maybe deep down, in the depths of my heart, I do care.

#28

I'M SURE GORDON realizes that by walking through this doorway he may be:

1. Crossing a line in Pete's head.

2. Dooming himself to be cursed, or worse.

Still, he:

1. Doesn't hesitate.

2. Smiles.

3. Says, "Thanks for letting me join in."

"Thank you for wanting to help," Cicely says.

"I just hope I'll be able to somehow."

"I'm sure you will. More heads are better than less. Well, except when you're born with two and your other head's narrow-minded and annoying."

"You're speaking from experience?" I say.

"I wish I weren't," Cicely says. "She and I never got along, so we decided to make a clean break. I went my way. She rolled hers. The last thing I heard, she was dating a bigoted bowling ball in Texas. Anyway, you two make yourselves at home. I'll finish up the nymph hair pasta. I hear it's even better than angel." She heads into the kitchen.

And I:

1. Lead Gordon to the couch.

2. Introduce him to Abby.

"What's your dog's name?" Abby says.

"Meta," Gordon says.

"Oh. That was the name one of the first guide dogs in Britain, right?"

He grins. "Yeah."

"Can I pet her?"

"Sure. Let me take off her harness first, so she knows it's party time."

While Gordon's busy with that, I move my chair away from the couch, to the opposite side of the room.

Abby stares at me.

"I don't want to hurt you anymore," I say. "Maybe if we don't get too close, we can keep our curses from mingling."

"Are you sure that'll work?" she says.

"No, but it's worth a try, right?"

"That's true."

"All done," Gordon says.

Then Abby:

  1. Pets Meta.

  2. Says, "Did you know a dog was King of Norway for 3 years?"

"I can't say that I did," Gordon says. "I take it you're a fan of our canine brothers and sisters?"

"Yeah. I'm more interested in arthropods though."

"I don't know much about insects, but I've always found fleas fascinating. You know they've caused more human deaths than all the wars ever fought, combined?"

"Yeah, people say fleas caused the Black Death, but I've read a lot of alternative theories. The Black Death could've been an Ebola-like virus or a form of anthrax, and not the bubonic plague at all. So maybe fleas had nothing to do with it. But even if the disease was spread by fleas, it wasn't their fault or anything. Terrible epidemics like that would never happen if humans weren't so overpopulated."

"Can't argue with that."

At this point, I decide to join Cicely in the kitchen.

"Can I help?" I say.

"I am in dire need of a taste tester," Cicely says, holding out a wooden spoon.

I taste. "Delicious. What is it?"

"Killer tomato soup."

"Seriously? How'd you manage to kill the killer tomatoes?"

"I went after the babies."

"That's a bit harsh, don't you think?"

"It's the circle of life, Nicholas. And circles are never wrong."

"That's true."

We carry the pasta and soup to the table.

"I asked Abby to move in last night," Cicely says.

Jealousy slaps me across the face, but still I say, "That's good. She's better off not living alone right now." And part of me is happy for her.

Because I've decided my jealousy has:

1. Nothing to do with hating Abby.
2. Everything to do with wanting time alone with Cicely.

During dinner, Abby:

1. Drops her spoon.
2. Bumps her head on the table.
3. Says, "That was my 4th head injury today. I only need 2 more before midnight and I'll break my all-time record."

"I have a bike helmet in the garage," Cicely says, standing.

"You can't protect me from the world, Cis."

"I can try."

"If I wore a helmet, I'd only get hit by something that much harder. You can't stop it."

"I'll just have to make Pete stop it then."

Suddenly, my whole body feels coated with ice.

And maybe I look as doom and gloomy as I feel, because Cicely says, "Of course, tracking Pete down is out of the question. Then again, that probably isn't the best way to go about confronting him anyway."

"What do you mean?" I say.

"We're almost positive that he spies on us. So if we do somehow figure out his location, he'll know that we know. And if he doesn't want to be found, he'll move somewhere else."

"You're probably right."

"So instead of searching him out, we need to find some way to draw him to us."

"That won't be easy," Gordon says. "Pete probably won't stray from his own plans if he feels like he's being manipulated. The whole reason he doesn't want us looking for him is because he wants to be the one in control."

"That makes sense," Cicely says.

"I'm not saying it's impossible. If we give him a good enough reason, he might show himself."

"What happens if we do face him?" Abby says.

"We stop him," Cicely says. "We make him undo our curses."

"What if we can't?"

"We have to try."

"Cicely's right," Gordon says. "Pete won't be happy with causing fear and suffering forever. I hate to say this, but if we don't find some way to stop him, he'll most likely end up progressing to murder."

"We don't know that for sure," Abby says. "Maybe he only wants to keep things the way they are."

Part of me wants to:

    1. Agree with Abby.

    2. Avoid another encounter with Pete.

Still, I say, "The way things are isn't safe. Your curse could kill you, Abby."

"Maybe not," Abby says. "Maybe it can only give me superficial wounds."

"I stabbed you with a knife."

"It wasn't a bad stabbing. The doctor said so."

"I understand your worries, hon," Cicely says. "There's a chance that confronting Pete would only make things worse." Then she holds out her tennis ball. "There's also a chance that I'm not a robot incapable of human error, and I'll drop this someday."

We all sit in silence for a few heartbeats.

The truth is, I:

    1. Don't usually feel frightened about Cicely and the ball.

    2. Feel safer with the world in her hands.

But Cicely's right. She can't hold on forever, and she shouldn't have to try.

"I don't doubt your experience, Cicely," Gordon says. "I'm just wondering if you've considered that the nature of your curse is self-deception."

And Cicely says, "You mean have I considered that instead of being responsible for the fate of the world, I'm being forced to believe that I am? A zillion times yes. But no matter how powerful my doubts, the truth remains lodged inside me like a giant kidney stone. I know it seems impossible that a ball could be so connected to the world, but doesn't Pete deal in impossibilities? None of us know the limits of his power, and personally, I'm not willing to drop the ball to find out." She stands. "Anyone have room for dessert?"

Later, while we're watching *Amelie*, the doorbell rings. I shiver, because I haven't been slapped yet today. And a few faces flicker in my mind.

1. John.
2. Greg.
3. Karl.
4. Pete.

But when Cicely opens the door, none of them are standing on the other side.

"Kin," Abby says.

"Ruth," Cicely says.

"Oh god," Ruth says, looking as surprised to see us as we are to see her. "I think I need to sit down."

"Of course."

I rush into the kitchen to retrieve another chair, and when I return, Ruth's:

1. Sitting on the couch, arms crossed.
2. Still as the mural behind her.

"Can I get you anything?" Cicely says.

Ruth shakes her head, then says, "When you came to visit me, you said I'd forgotten you. All three of you."

"That's right."

"I didn't believe you, of course. Then I started seeing things. Little things. Flashes. I thought that by the power of suggestion, my mind was creating false memories so that it seemed like I did know you. I live alone, and I thought this was a defense mechanism for loneliness. But this house is exactly the way I remember it. I remember the mural. I remember eating here with all of you. Except you and the dog." She glances at Gordon.

"We're new," Gordon says

"I think I vomited on someone," Ruth says.

"That was me," I say.

"I remember another house too," Ruth says, and turns to Abby. "I was lying on a couch, and you were reading to me from a book."

"I used to read to you a lot," Abby says, tears on her cheeks. "We were good friends when you were Kin."

"I don't understand any of this."

"You used to be someone else," Cicely says. "Kin had a different personality, different memories. We thought a man named Pete destroyed her, but apparently she still exists somewhere inside you."

"If you're saying I'm really Kin, then who's Ruth?"

"Pete said he created you."

Ruth winces. And so do I.

Somehow, I expected Cicely to keep this information from Ruth.

"So I'm not real," Ruth says.

"You're real," Cicely says. "Your memories as Ruth may be fabricated or manipulated, but Pete could've lied about creating you. Maybe you have the same soul as Kin, or maybe he put a new soul into Kin's body."

"I don't believe in souls."

"I'm sorry."

Then Ruth:

1. Stands.

2. Wipes away an escaped tear.

3. Says, "This can't be happening. It's not happening. For all I know, I broke into someone's house and I'm talking to empty space right now. I should go."

"We're not hallucinations," Cicely says.

"If I get sucked in by my own delusions, I may never find my way out. God, I should have known I was going insane when I found this house by chance. Things like that don't happen in reality."

"What do you mean by chance?"

Ruth:

1. Stares at the door for a few moments.

2. Sits again.

3. Says, "Sometimes I drive around town to relax. Today, I wandered by your house, and recognized the outside from one of my flashes. I wasn't looking for you. I had no idea where this house was located. If this is real, then I'm here because of blind luck."

"Maybe not. Kin was able to connect with the world on a deep level. It's possible that if her memories are returning, her abilities are reawakening as well. Maybe that's how you found us."

"What the hell are you talking about?"

"Kin was psychic," Abby says.

Ruth:

1. Stares at the door again.

2. Says, "Can I have a glass of water?"

"Ice or no ice?" Cicely says.

"No ice."

"I'll be right back."

In Cicely's absence, silence overtakes the room.

Gordon and Abby busy themselves petting Meta while Ruth stares at her hands.

And me, I consider the possibility that:

1. It wasn't luck or Kin's 6th sense that brought Ruth here today.

2. My curse orchestrated this reunion.

3. Ruth's destined to slap me.

But I don't tell anyone this.

Instead, I study my mole until Cicely returns.

Then Ruth:

1. Gulps down all the water.

2. Stares inside the empty cup.

"Can I get you anything else?" Cicely says.

"No," Ruth says.

And silence saturates the room again.

Finally, Ruth:

1. Sets the cup down.
2. Turns to Cicely.
3. Says, "If I'm not insane, then the world is. I don't know how to handle that."

"We'll help you," Cicely says.

Ruth releases a sharp snicker. "I'm sorry for laughing, but I don't see how anyone can help me."

"I understand, hon. I felt the same way at first."

"What? You became a different person too?"

"No, but he cursed me. He cursed all of us, except Gordon."

"But Gordon's cursed too," Abby says. "In a way."

"Jesus fuck," Gordon says. "Just because I'm not sighted doesn't mean I'm suffering some tragedy."

Abby:

1. Looks like she's about to cry.
2. Says, soft, "I'm sorry. I just thought it might be hard not to see."

"Being blind isn't always easy," Gordon says. "But that has way more to do with how the world perceives me than how my body perceives the world. More often than not, I'm seen as some useless, sexless, pathetic creature that can't possibly have a full life. So if you want to empathize with me for how horribly I'm treated on a regular basis, go ahead. Just don't pity me for not fitting into some socially constructed mold of normality. It's insulting."

"I'm sorry."

"Thank you." Gordon sighs. "I'm sorry for swearing at you. I shouldn't've talked to you that way."

"It's alright."

"I have a daughter," Ruth says, her voice breaking. "If I spoke to her, would she remember me? Or would she remember Kin?"

"I don't know," Cicely says.

"Oh god, do I even have a daughter? She could be a manufactured memory, couldn't she?"

"Kin has a daughter," Abby says. "Maybe Pete incorporated her into your memories."

"Is her name Rita?" Ruth says.

Abby nods.

And Ruth:

1. Stands.

2. Says, "Can I call her? Somewhere private?"

3. Heads into the bedroom after Cicely points the way.

Then Cicely:

1. Taps the tennis ball against her forehead.

2. Turns to Abby.

3. Says, "I don't know why I didn't think of this before. What if Pete did to your family exactly what he did to Kin? They could be out there, somewhere, with new memories and new lives."

"That's true," Abby says.

"And if they are like Ruth, their old selves could still exist inside them. They might start remembering who they are."

Abby smiles a little. "Yeah."

A short time later, Ruth:

1. Returns with puffy eyes.

2. Says, "She remembers me. Why does she remember me as Ruth and you all remember me as Kin?"

And Cicely says, "Pete violated Kin's identity in order to threaten us. He'll do the same thing to me if we start searching for him again."

"You're saying this happened to me because someone wanted to scare you?"

"Yes."

Suddenly, grim fury gnarls Ruth's face, and for a moment I'm afraid she's going to:

1. Blame us.

2. Attack Cicely.

I stand.

"Pete," Ruth says. "Who is he?"

"We don't even know what he is," Abby says.

"Whatever he is, he's a psychopath," Gordon says.

"You don't have any memories of him?" Cicely says. "From when he changed you?"

"No," Ruth says.

Then I:

    1. Take out my purple notebook.

    2. Show my drawing of the smirking face to Ruth.

    3. Say, "This is him."

"I want to know what he's done to you," Ruth says. "All of you."

So we tell her.

And I'm afraid after everything she's gone through, our stories will overwhelm her with despair.

But after we finish, Ruth appears close to calm.

"I'm sorry," Ruth says. "I feel sick to think I'm so connected with this brute. I hope he didn't put any of himself in me when he made me who I am."

"He didn't," Cicely says, as if she can somehow see the truth in Ruth's eyes. Maybe she can.

Ruth sighs with what must be relief, because her frown wanes afterward. "If you ever need my help in stopping him, let me know. I should warn you first, I'm a terrible Good Samaritan. No matter what my intentions are, I have a tendency to hurt more than help."

"Hon, you're only remembering what Pete put in your mind. I'm sure you're capable of much more than you imagine. Heck, you've already helped us."

"Have I?"

"You've shown us that Pete's capable of making mistakes. He worked hard to remove evidence of Kin from the world. He altered your memories, Rita's, and probably the memories of everyone you know. But it wasn't enough. Kin's still stirring inside you, and I don't think he planned for that. What I'm not sure about is whether he thought he could erase someone from reality and failed, or if he was exaggerating his abilities and didn't expect us to find out."

"I'm guessing the latter," Gordon says. "He could've threatened you with something he's fully capable of doing. But in all likelihood, Pete's a pathological liar. I'm sure he wants to convince us he's more powerful than he is."

"But he is powerful," Abby says. "Why would he need to lie about it?"

Gordon rubs his chin. "He could be the most powerful man on earth, and he'll still want to come off as some sort of god."

"What if he is one?"

"He's not," Cicely says, firm.

"I think Pete's a coward," I say. "The only time I've ever had direct contact with him, he had me chained to a wall. And most of the time, he sneaks around leaving us little notes. That reminds me. Ruth, when I came to your house the other day, did you see anyone near my car?"

"No," Ruth says.

"I'm asking because Pete left a note on my windshield while I was talking to you. It's possible he made his move while I was walking up the driveway, but I think it's more likely that he can camouflage himself somehow. Make himself invisible. That might even explain how he spies on us."

"You're saying he just watches us from inside our homes?" Abby says.

"Maybe," I say. "The point is, I doubt there was ever any chance of us finding him. If he doesn't want to be seen, he won't be seen."

"But Pete said he would hurt Cicely if we kept looking for him. Why would he make that threat if we can't find him? You think he was just trying to scare us?"

"No, I'm sure he'll hurt any or all of us if we break his rule. But I don't think he threatened us to keep us from finding him. I think he's afraid that in the process of searching for him, we might discover who and what he is. Gordon's right about him. Pete wants us to think he's more than he is, so he lies constantly and creates a mystique for himself. He hides behind the illusion that he's some supreme being. And I think he's trying to deceive himself with this fantasy as much as he is us. Because without the self-delusion, he'd have to face how screwed up and out of control he really is."

I don't tell them I'm speaking from experience.

What I do say is, "He's so afraid of being seen as the pathetic creature he is, I doubt he'll ever show himself to us again. Like I said, he's a coward."

Abby looks around the room.

Then Ruth:

  1. Stands.

  2. Says, "I'm tired. I'd better head home."

"You can come back anytime," Cicely says.

"Thank you for everything. All of you."

Ruth:

  1. Shakes hands with Cicely and Gordon.

  2. Walks over to Abby.

  2. Steps on Abby's bare foot, causing Abby to yelp.

  4. Stumbles backwards.

And I:

  1. Rush forward.

  2. Steady Ruth from behind.

  3. Feel #28 on my cheek after Ruth spins around.

But it's not really me she's attacking.

"I thought you were him," Ruth says, shaking. "I'm sorry."

"It's alright," I say. "I understand."

Ruth finishes her:

  1. Apologies.

  2. Goodbyes.

Then as soon as the front door closes, Abby's emotions pour out of her in raspy sobs.

I put my arm around her, because:

  1. I'm the closest to her.

  2. I'm no more likely to hurt her than anyone else right now, since I've been slapped.

  3. I want to.

"Everything's gonna be alright," I say.

Abby:

1. Wipes off her face.
2. Says, "I'm just so happy about Kin, you know? I thought she was dead. But maybe she's coming back."

"Maybe," I say.

"I have these books at my house. They're Kin's favorites, and I used to read them to her all the time. Do you think if I gave them to her, it might help her remember more times we spent together?"

"It's worth a try."

"I think I'll go get them. Thanks, Nick." She:

1. Hugs me.
2. Walks toward the door.

"Do you want me to go with you?" Cicely says.

"I'll be alright," Abby says.

"Meta's ready to go home," Gordon says. "Abby, would you mind dropping us off on your way? I don't want to force Nick to leave before he's ready, if I can help it."

"I don't mind driving you," I say.

"I can do it," Abby says. "It's no problem or anything."

"Thanks," Gordon says, and begins to put the harness on Meta.

Abby bites her fingernail. "I'm really sorry about what I said before. I feel really bad."

"I never wanted you to feel bad. I wanted you to hear me out about why I felt offended, and you did. You don't have to keep apologizing."

"I'm sorry."

"How about we drop the subject, and you tell me more about your favorite bugs."

Abby smiles.

When they're gone, I take my usual spot on the couch.

Cicely, hers.

Then she stands and says, "On second thought, I should go visit flushie. He gets lonely if I ignore him for too long."

So while Cicely's in the bathroom, my mind wanders back to Pete. I think about him lurking in this house, watching Cicely as she:

1. Sleeps.

2. Undresses.

3. Showers.

He could be watching her right now.

Suddenly, rage grips my jaws and hands, and won't let go.

Cicely:

1. Returns.

2. Sits beside me, close.

3. Says, "I'm tired of thinking about the curses. Maybe for tonight we could pretend we're normal weirdoes, with normal problems. Sound good?"

"Sounds good," I say, and take a deep breath.

"Do you want to finish the movie? Or we could talk more."

"Let's talk."

And so we do.

We talk about:

1. Marshmallow Peeps that time travel to the Mesozoic Era.

2. Tooth fairies who embezzle gold fillings from sleeping adults.

3. Coconut monkeys that participate in Civil War reenactments.

4. Our happiest memories.

5. Our most ridiculous and wonderful hopes and dreams.

On and on.

And maybe I don't deserve such a fairy tale evening.

But at this point, I don't care.

#29

IN MY DREAM, everyone's lying on the floor, covered with blood. I'm trying to tell them how sorry I am that I didn't burn up the beast when I had the chance, but they can't hear me. Or maybe they're ignoring me.

I can't see outside the window with all the boards in the way.

Then everyone's bodies contort. They kick and punch at the air and mouth words I can't hear.

My mind clears.

And I know I can't escape this nightmare.

I'm already awake.

"Oh god," I say.

Cicely, Gordon, Ruth, they:

1. Stop moving.

2. Open their eyes.

3. Sit up.

Ruth shrieks.

"Something's wrong with Abby," Cicely says, because Abby's still convulsing on the floor.

"You were all doing that," I say. "Maybe I was too, before I woke up."

"Whose blood is this?" Ruth says, holding her red hands out to Cicely. "Am I bleeding?"

Then I:

1. Remember my bathroom sink full of fake blood.

2. Smell my hands.

3. Lick my finger.

    4. Say, "I don't think this is blood."

"What's going on?" Abby says, sitting up, finally.

Cicely:

    1. Smiles.

    2. Hugs her.

    3. Says, "We don't know, hon."

"Why is there so much blood?" Abby says.

"We don't think it's real."

"Where are we?" Gordon says.

I glance around and say, "A big room. The walls are made of logs."

"We're in a log cabin?"

"Maybe."

"Is Meta here?"

"No."

And Gordon:

    1. Stands.

    2. Walks toward the wall.

    3. Recoils his hands, yelling.

    4. Stumbles back.

"Are you alright?" I say, rushing beside him.

"Get me out of here!" Gordon says.

"What happened?"

Gordon:

    1. Squeezes my arm, tight.

    2. Says, "It's gonna kill me, Nick!"

Then Ruth:

    1. Races toward the door.

    2. Stops, screaming.

    3. Turns around.

    4. Staggers to Cicely.

    5. Collapses.

    6. Curls up.

7. Covers her face with her hands.

8. Cries.

"Are you OK?" Cicely says.

"Help me," Ruth says, through her fingers.

"How do you want me to help you, hon?"

"I don't know."

Cicely puts her free hand on Ruth's shoulder.

"Please take me outside," Gordon says, his voice breaking.

"I want to," I say. "But it seems like something's happening when we get close to the walls or the door. You were both about a yard away when you yelled. Maybe we should stay here for now."

Gordon rubs his chin. "You're probably right."

"Did something hurt you?"

"Yeah."

"Where?"

Gordon holds out his hands.

I examine them. They're:

1. Red.

2. Shaking.

"Here," Abby says, handing me a water bottle. "There's a bunch of them in that box over there."

"Thanks," I say. "I'm gonna wash off your hands, Gordon."

"Wait!" Gordon says. "What if it's poisoned?"

"I already drank some," Abby says. "I don't feel sick at all."

Gordon sighs. "Alright. Wash them off."

So I do.

Then I:

1. Study his hands again, slow and careful.

2. Say, "I don't see anything wrong with them."

And Cicely says, "I can't find any marks on Ruth either."

"What part of your hands are hurting, Gordon?"

"My hands feel fine," Gordon says. "To be honest, the attack wasn't that bad.

All the pain disappeared the moment I moved away from the wall. After that, I just freaked out. It seems ridiculous now, but for a while I was sure some big creature was gonna…well…eat me. I'm sorry I panicked."

"Don't you always tell me not to apologize for my feelings?"

"Yeah. Still, I'm sorry for squeezing your arm."

"It's alright." I turn to Cicely. "How's Ruth doing?"

"She's terrified," Cicely says.

"Of a big animal?"

"I don't know."

"What if it's Pete?" Abby says. "What if he's in here with us?"

Ruth cries harder.

And I scan the room.

"We might want to arm ourselves," Gordon says. "If there's anything to arm ourselves with, that is."

"There's this," Abby says, picking up a hammer.

"He's going to kill us," Ruth says.

"No one's going to kill anyone," Cicely says.

"Maybe he left us a note," I say.

"I hope so," Gordon says. "But I doubt he trapped us in some secluded area to talk. We are in the middle of nowhere, aren't we?"

"I don't know. The windows are all boarded up."

"There's some lanterns in here too," Abby says. "They're made of metal. We could swing them, you know?"

"Good," Gordon says. "We should all probably sit back to back, in the center of the room. That way, we'd only have one side to defend."

"Should I pass out the weapons?"

"Yeah."

After Abby hands me a lantern, I:

    1. Search the room for a note, keeping my distance from the walls.

    2. Clutch onto the hope that Pete didn't bring us here to die.

But all can I find is:

    1. A box of nails.

2. Rope.

3. Duct tape.

4. More water bottles.

5. Permanent markers.

6. Wigs.

I don't want to give up yet, so I look over the room again.

And my eyes pause on Cicely. She:

1. Unwraps the duct tape from her tennis ball hand.

2. Grimaces as she flexes her fingers.

For a moment, I hate Pete for wrapping her hand so tight.

Then I realize Cicely must do this to herself every evening, to keep the world safe while she sleeps.

I can't help but imagine Pete:

1. Sneaking into her room in the middle of the night.

2. Dragging her out of bed.

3. Changing her clothes.

4. Carrying her to his car.

Finally, the obvious hits me.

"Would you all mind checking your clothes?" I say.

They check.

I end up finding the letter in the first place I look.

"I have it," I say. "Should I read it out loud?"

"Yeah," Gordon says.

So I read:

Dear Everybody,

I hope you're in the mood for a bloody massacre, because in a couple minutes, I'm going to kill you all.

No, I just wanted to see if I could make any of you crap your pants. Seriously though, whether or not you survive this experience depends entirely on your performance here today. But before we get into all that, I need to clarify a few things.

First of all, Nicky, I know you were trying to entice me to reveal myself by calling me a coward yesterday. It was a good plan, but it had some flaws.

1. I have absolutely no need to prove myself to a petty underling like you.
2. Like I told you before, I'm the one who gets what he wants. Not you.
3. I'm not a fucking retard.

So you failed again, buddy. I'm sure you're not surprised.

Another thing, your invisibility idea is dead wrong. Sure, I have the ability to sneak around your houses like some brainless chameleon, but I'd find that a little degrading. I prefer watching you all from the comfort of my own home. That way, I can focus on the TV when your mundane lives start to bore me to death.

And I hate to tell you this, but you're not the only people who I keep tabs on. There are thousands of you out there. I'm sorry if that makes you feel less special.

But in all honesty, you are some of my favorite projects. I wouldn't take the time to write you such a long letter otherwise. And I certainly wouldn't have gone out of my way to meet you in person, Nicky. You're a very special person, and you're doing me proud.

Still, you should all give up hope that any of you will ever see me in person. I'm a very busy being, and I hardly ever leave this room. I leave most of my grunt work to my children.

That's right, Ruth. You're not an only child. You have siblings all over the planet. For instance, it was one of your bird brothers who put the letter on Nicky's windshield right outside your house.

And by the way, Ruth, you were the one who brought everyone here today.

You boarded up the windows, and you activated the barrier in the cabin by saying a very special word. I'm telling you this, because I want you to know that once you join my family, there's no getting out. Kin's never coming back. Your free will is finito.

Cicely, I know you believe Kin's soul still exists inside Ruth. That's a sweet sentiment, but there's no such thing as souls. There's nothing eternal about you humans. That's why you're called mortals.

The only reason there's still a few of Kin's memories inside Ruth is because I left a few crumbs when I devoured her.

As for you, Abby, I don't want you to **hold** onto any false hopes concerning your family, because that would be cruel. The **truth** is, I swallowed them whole, body and mind. There's nothing left of them **anywhere**, and there never will be.

Now that we have that out of the way, let's talk survival. As I already mentioned, there's a barrier in the cabin. I could try to explain the nature of this barrier to you, but none of you have the intelligence to understand, so I'm not going to waste my time.

All you need to know is that you can't cross the barrier. If you go too far into it, you'll pass out from the pain. And there's no point trying to go above or below it, because it's spherical. The only way you're getting out of there is if the barrier breaks. And that won't happen until the door opens. And the door won't open until you complete the list of tasks on the other side of this parchment.

Kind regards,
Pete.

P.S. Gordon, I'd be remiss if I didn't address you at least once in this letter, since you're now an official member of the club. I know you think you have me all figured out, but you don't. Remember when you told Nicky serial killers never become the gods they imagine themselves to be? Well, that may be true, but you're dealing with the god of serial killers and psychopaths. I'm Jesus's long lost evil twin.

P.P.S. The barrier eats fire, so don't waste your time trying to burn down the door. And FYI, even if the barrier wasn't fireproof and you tried burning your way out, you'd end up killing yourselves in the process anyway.

P.P.P.S. I forgot to mention, you'll find all the necessary items for today's performance in the cardboard box Ruth prepared for you. And remember, you each have to participate, or your actions will have no effect on the cabin door. Break a leg.

After staring at the letter for a while, I:

    1. Flip the paper over.

    2. Read through the list of tasks.

    3. Imagine my friends doing all this for Pete's amusement.

"What does it say?" Gordon says.

"It doesn't matter," I say, crumpling up the to-do list. "We're not doing what he wants. We're gonna find another way out."

"What if there is no other way?" Abby says, crying.

Suddenly, I see a blur of motion in the corner of my eye. So I:

    1. Tighten my grip on the lantern.

    2. Look around.

    3. Listen hard.

    4. Will myself to be Batman.

But the bloody massacre I'm imagining doesn't begin.

And I spot a moth on the wall.

"He doesn't look affected by the barrier," I say, pointing.

"Maybe it only works on us," Gordon says.

"Maybe that's one of Pete's children," Cicely says.

Then Ruth:

    1. Sits up.

    2. Rubs her eyes.

    3. Says, "I'm sorry. I didn't mean to bring you all here. I don't remember any of it."

"It's not your fault," Cicely says.

"I know. I'm a puppet."

"You're more than that, Ruth. I don't care what Pete says. He's a liar."

"I hope you're wrong."

"What do you mean?"

Ruth looks down at her lap. "If Pete's telling the truth, then I'm safe. This is going to sound heartless, but I don't want Kin coming back. I don't want her to take over my body and make me into nothing. I know I'm only a pawn in Pete's game, and I know Kin deserves existence more than I do, but I don't want to die."

Cicely puts on hand on Ruth's. "Your life's just as important as anyone else's."

"I appreciate the thought, Cicely, but it's not true. The price of my creation was too high." She turns to Abby. "You lost a good friend, and my daughter lost her real mother. All Rita has left are memories of me, and those aren't worth remembering. I never treated her very well." Tears escape Ruth's face again. "I know there's nothing I can do to make up for the loss of Kin. But I'll do everything I can not to waste the life I've been given. I'll be a good friend to you, Abby. I'll try. Would you like to be friends?"

Abby:

    1. Weeps, soft.

    2. Nods.

I turn to Ruth and say, "If you don't mind me asking, what happened when you approached the door? Understanding the barrier might help us find a way out."

"I started reliving memories," Ruth says.

"Kin's memories?" Abby says.

"No. Mine. I don't want to go into details, but I will say they were the worst moments from my childhood. Of course, it's freeing in a way, knowing that my past isn't real. Still, the memories feel real enough, and experiencing them is… dispiriting, to say the least."

And I can't think of anything else to say but, "I'm sorry."

Ruth stares at the floor.

Then I say, "Gordon. When you touched the barrier, did you connect with some event from your childhood?"

"I don't think so," Gordon says. "Unless I was hunted by a giant Gila monster at some point, and I forgot. Sorry. I shouldn't be joking right now."

"It's alright. Have you ever feared being eaten before?"

"Not that I can remember. Sorry."

At this point, I decide to test what Pete said about fire. So I:

1. Tie the rope to my lantern.
2. Inch the lantern toward the barrier with the hammer.
3. Watch the flame swirl faster and faster until going out.
4. Pull the lantern back to me.

Time ticks on, and the only escape plan I come up with involves:

1. Tying the rope to the hammer.
2. Throwing the hammer at the door.
3. Retrieving the hammer with the rope.
4. Throwing the hammer again.

On and on.

But the door remains as solid and closed as ever.

And really, I'm not surprised.

Under Pete's control, Ruth probably:

1. Removed the handle from the door.
2. Barricaded the door on the outside.
3. Climbed in through the window.
4. Boarded up the windows.
5. Activated the barrier.

"I don't think this is gonna work," I say, dragging the hammer back to me for the 50th time.

"It was a good idea," Gordon says.

I don't agree, but I don't tell him that.

Instead, I say, "Thanks."

At this point, Ruth breaks her hours of silence, saying, "Could you tell me about her?"

"Kin?" Abby says.

"Yes. But if it's too painful…"

"I don't mind." Abby sits up straight, as if this'll help her remember. Maybe it will. "She liked animals and books. And spending time with people. I don't know what she didn't like, because she never talked about stuff like that, you know? Though I guess I know she didn't like to criticize things. She was kind and friendly. Whenever I spent time with her, she made me feel like I was really special. Like there was nowhere else in the world she'd rather be."

"Thank you."

Abby:

    1. Smiles.

    2. Cries.

I set down my hammer, and say, "I'm gonna try to open the door."

Everyone turns to look at me, except Gordon.

"Pete said you'd pass out," Abby says.

"Pete's a liar," I say. "And even if he's telling the truth about the barrier, maybe I can run and push open the door before I pass out. Maybe I only have to open it a little."

"You can't," Ruth says. "The pain's too much."

I stand. "I need to try."

"Wait, hon," Cicely says. "What if the barrier's more dangerous than Pete implied?"

"If anything, I think he's more likely to exaggerate the threat."

"Please, Nicholas," Cicely says, crackles. "What if it kills you?"

"It won't."

Of course, there's no way I can possibly know that.

But at this point, I don't care.

I run.

By the time I regain consciousness, I feel:

    1. Naked.

    2. Empty.

    3. Alone.

I want to:

    1. Turn myself invisible.

    2. Bury myself alive.

    3. Remove myself from existence.

But this is the same old story about a person's past, and how there's nowhere else to hide.

The barrier ripped me open like a stuffed animal.

And now my friends are my enemies, because they can see:

    1. The things I've done.

    2. The secrets I've kept.

    3. The real me.

"Don't hurt me," I say.

"No one's going to hurt you, hon," Cicely says. She's wearing a mask of compassion, but I can see the grim fury underneath.

"Don't do this. Please."

Then she:

    1. Puts her hand on my cheek, soft.

    2. Burns me with the fury emanating from her skin.

    3. Says, "You're safe, Nicholas."

Suddenly, I understand why Cicely never slapped me. This phenomenon had:

    1. Nothing to do with some special bond between us.

    2. Everything to do with conserving all her hatred for the end.

All I can do now is:

    1. Cry.

    2. Beg.

    3. Wait.

So I do.

Obviously, I know my pleading won't stop the inevitable.

This is what I deserve.

"Nothing will help him," Ruth says. "Except time."

And Gordon says, "I think it's safe to assume the barrier makes us each feel vulnerable in some way."

"I want to go home," I say. I'm not speaking about:

1. My apartment.
2. Sol's house.
3. Anywhere I can remember.

"You'll feel better soon, Nick," Gordon says.

He's right.

In a few minutes, I:

1. Sit up.
2. Wipe my eyes.
3. Say, "What happened?"

"You collapsed in the barrier," Cicely says. "I pulled you out."

"Thank you." I smile at her, but she doesn't smile back. "How long was I unconscious?"

"Hours."

"Did I touch the door?"

"No."

"Was I close?"

"No."

"I'm sorry," I say, meaning I'm:

1. Not only sorry for failing.
2. Apologizing for entering the barrier when I knew how much this would hurt her.

Then Cicely says, "Maybe we should do what Pete wants."

The words claw into my chest, breaking my heart.

"We can't," I say.

"Fighting back's only going to make things worse," Cicely says. "That's all it's ever done."

"We'll find another way out."

"I think Cis is right," Abby says. "Where's that list?"

And I:

    1. Remove the lump of paper from my sock.

    2. Squeeze the list, tight.

"What does he want us to do?" Cicely says.

"It doesn't matter," I say. "The door'll only open if we all participate. And I won't."

"I understand your feelings, hon. But if we don't get out of here, we're going to run out of water and die."

"We'll escape before that happens."

Cicely sighs. "We've never broken one of Pete's curses. What makes you think we can free ourselves from his barrier?"

"I don't know."

My grip loosens.

"Oh fuck," Gordon says. "I may have an idea."

"An escape idea?" I say.

"Yeah. But it's probably not gonna work, so don't get your hopes up."

I don't say, "Too late."

Gordon:

    1. Rubs his forehead.

    2. Says, "Pete said the barrier will break when the door opens, right?"

"Right," I say.

"So what if we get someone to open the door from the outside? According to Pete, the barrier exists inside the cabin, so there's a chance the person outside wouldn't be affected."

"That's possible, but I'm sure Pete planned for that. For one, we're probably in the middle of nowhere. And even if there are people around, the windows are boarded up so nobody can see us. The barrier might even block out sound."

"Don't worry, Nick. My plan isn't to scream for help. I know Pete would've anticipated that. But maybe he didn't plan for everything." He scratches his eyebrow. "You haven't been slapped yet today, have you?"

"I don't think so. Unless I was slapped in bed, or when I was being moved here. But I doubt the curse works on me when I'm asleep or unconscious. I wouldn't suffer enough that way."

"Good. So we just need your curse to bring in somebody from outside."

"I wish it worked like that, Gordon, but it's more likely one of you will slap me. Especially with the way my curse and Abby's curse hone in on each other."

"That's where the rope comes in."

"Oh."

After everyone agrees to try out Gordon's plan, I:

    1. Start on Gordon.

    2. Feel sick.

    3. Say, "Is this too tight?"

"It's not tight enough," Gordon says. "Also, I don't think tying our hands is enough. Our fingers are still free. And if we're able to untie each other's ropes, the curse will probably manipulate the situation so that we have to free someone."

"Why would you have to free someone?"

"I don't know. To keep that person from dying, maybe. In any case, you need to make it as impossible as possible for us to slap you, so your curse will give up on us and target someone else."

I want to disagree, but of course Gordon's right. "I'll duct tape your hands."

"You'd better tape up our feet too. Just in case."

"Alright."

"There's also our teeth to worry about."

"You want me to duct tape your mouths too?"

"Want probably isn't the best word, but yeah. That should help."

"Is everyone alright with this?"

They are.

So I carry on.

And with every knot, my heart sinks a little farther.

"I'm sorry," I say, binding Cicely's hands behind her. "This isn't nearly as horrible as what Pete wanted us to do, but it's still horrible. I wish there was a better way."

"It's alright, hon," Cicely says, so soft I can barely hear her. "I'm fine."

Doom and gloomy tears flee from my eyes.

"Jesus fuck," Gordon says. "I was so focused on making us harmless, I forgot about you. Nick, if you're not tied up, the curse will probably create a scenario where you'll be compelled to free one of us."

"I know," I say.

"Maybe you can pinion yourself somehow."

"I'll see what I can do."

Countless tears later, I:

1. Finish taping up Cicely's mouth.
2. Toss the tape back into the box. Not out of courtesy, but habit.
3. Take the to-do list out of my sock, because I don't want Pete's message touching me anymore.
4. Read #3 again, which is, "Line up, crotch to ass. Then tie yourselves together and walk around the room like a giant maggot. This one's for you, Abby. I know how much you love creepy crawlers."
5. Glance at #8.
6. Feel nauseous.
7. Throw the paper on the floor.
8. Step on it.
9. Look at my friends.
10. Say, "I don't think I can secure myself on my own. Anyway, there isn't much tape left. I'm sorry, Cicely."

With her eyes, she begs me not to go.

But I do.

And the fear and the pain swirl around inside me.

And for an instant I wonder which one will end up killing me.

Then I scream.

My heart thumps, hard.

I try to restrain myself, but hope for a fairy tale ending swells inside me.

I imagine my mother stepping through the doorway.

Then she hugs me tight.

She's beaming, crying, saving me, finally.

But it's:

    1. Not my mother.

    2. Svetlana.

She:

    1. Smiles.

    2. Says, "Uncle Nicky, were you sleeping on the floor?"

And I:

    1. Smile back.

    2. Say, "Sort of. I'm glad you're here, Svetlana."

She hands me a doorstop.

Then Greg and Nadia burst into the cabin, breathing hard.

"I don't know why you're here," I say. "But thank you."

"Nicky?" Nadia says.

I approach them, and Greg:

    1. Slaps me.

    2. Pushes me onto the floor.

    3. Lifts his flashlight like a club.

    4. Says, "Stay down."

Nadia:

    1. Limps over to Svetlana.

    2. Squeezes her arms.

    3. Says, "What are you doing to these people, Nicky?"

"Nothing," I say.

"Right," Greg says. "So they all bound and gagged themselves?"

"I was trapped here with them. Let me free them, and they'll tell you."

"You do it, Nadia. I'll make sure he doesn't move."

"Stand behind Daddy," Nadia says. "Then close your eyes and cover your ears."

"Why?" Svetlana says.

"Now."

Svetlana obeys.

Then Nadia:

    1. Stares at me for a few moments.

    2. Walks over to Ruth.

    3. Uncovers her mouth.

    4. Says, "Did he hurt you?"

"Nicholas helped save us," Ruth says.

"Oh."

"You can lower your weapon now," I say.

After a few seconds of glaring, Greg complies.

And I rush over to Cicely.

"Why is Uncle Nicky's friends all tied up?" Svetlana says.

"Your mother told you to cover your eyes," Greg says.

"Are you OK, hon?" Cicely says, the moment her mouth's free.

"Yeah," I say.

"You were in there so long. You kept convulsing. Are you sure you're OK?"

"I'm fine. Really. I didn't even feel paranoid when I woke up this time. The breaking of the barrier must've undone its effects on me."

Cicely sighs with what must be relief, because her brow relaxes a little afterward.

"I tied these too tight," I say, when I see the state of Cicely's wrists. "I'm sorry."

"It's not your fault," Cicely says. "I was struggling."

I almost ask her why, but then I:

    1. Realize the obvious.

    2. Feel dizzy with guilt.

Out of the corner of my eye, I see a flash.

"I'm sorry," Greg says.

"Don't worry about it," Abby says.

"What happened?" Nadia says.

And Greg says, "My flashlight slipped out of my hands and landed on her foot."

"Be more careful, Greg."

"I'm always careful."

At this point, Svetlana:

    1. Walks up beside me.

    2. Says, "Do you want to see my tent? I have a purple sleeping bag."

"I'd love to see everything," I say. "But I'm feeling really sleepy. I need to go home soon."

"Oh."

"Can I have a hug, Svetlana?"

"OK."

We hug.

"Thank you for saving me," I say.

"You're welcome," she says.

As soon as everyone's free, we rush out of the cabin. And my whole body feels lighter the instant I pass through the doorway.

"Good plan, Gordon," I say.

"Good guts, Nick," Gordon says, squeezing my arm.

Greg:

1. Points his flashlight at my chest.

2. Says, "Do you need us to stay and talk with the police?"

"You can go," I say. "We'll handle it."

Then Nadia:

1. Holds Svetlana's shoulders.

2. Says, "Don't you ever run away from Mommy and Daddy again. We need to stay very close when we're camping."

"But I had a bad dream," Svetlana says. "Uncle Nicky was stuck in the Jell-O."

"Nightmares are no reason to run away. If I didn't wake up when you were leaving the tent, you could've got lost in the woods."

"Like Hansel?"

"This isn't a story, Svetlana. Mommy hurt her ankle running after you. Did you know that?"

Svetlana:

1. Shakes her head.

2. Cries.

And Nadia:

1. Says, "Let's go, Greg."

2. Turns to me.

3. Says, "Goodbye, Nicky."

"Bye," I say.

Greg picks up Svetlana, and the three of them fade into the dark forest. As for the rest of us, we:

    1. Enter Ruth's car.

    2. Buckle up.

    3. Head for home.

"I hope Meta's alright," Gordon says.

"I'm sure she's fine," I say. But of course I'm not sure at all.

"If Pete hurt her, I'm gonna kill him."

Then Abby says, "Do you think Pete's mad about us getting out?"

"Yeah," I say.

"What do you think he's gonna do?"

"I don't know, but it doesn't matter. We're gonna find a way to stop him."

Somehow, I expect Cicely to:

    1. Break the silence that follows my words.

    2. Support my conviction.

In other words, I expect her to be her old self again.

But when I face her, she seems:

    1. Distant.

    2. Drained.

"Are you alright?" I say.

"No," she says, staring at the tennis ball in her hands.

"What's wrong?"

She laughs a little. "Everything's wrong, hon. Like you said, what we did to ourselves wasn't as horrible as Pete's list, but it was still horrible. Even when we win, we lose. Pete's going to keep putting us in cages, and eventually he'll find one we can't get out of."

Her words sink deep inside me.

And I try to believe:

    1. Cicely's wrong.

    2. We can escape this nightmare.

But part of me knows we're more than cursed.

We're doomed.

#30

CICELY HANDS Me a letter, so out loud I read:

Dear comrades,

Congratulations on your brilliant break out yesterday. Not only did you outplay me in my own game, you taught me a very valuable life lesson. I learned that despite your extreme imperfections, you humans deserve a little respect after all. In light of this realization, I've decided to undo your curses and grant each of you everlasting autonomy.

No, but seriously, I bet my buddy Steve that you'd figure out the alternate method of opening the door. He was positive you didn't have the brainpower, so I ended up winning 200 new minions. Thanks for that.

And you all deserve a big bravo for putting on such a delightful show. I haven't laughed so hard in weeks.

Best wishes,
Pete.

P.S. Nicky, I must commend you on delivering what was, to me, the stand out performance of the night. I especially enjoyed the scene where you so nobly surrendered yourself to suffering in order save your friends. Quite the Hallmark moment.

P.P.S. Also, Nicky, you should know that by remaining in the barrier so long, you allowed my awareness to seep deep inside you. Naturally, I took this opportunity to thoroughly explore your being, and truth be told, you're even more like me than I imagined. Your power is nothing compared to mine, of course, but your true nature is certainly impressive. Anyway, see you in the funny pages.

"He's just trying to fuck with your head, Nick," Gordon says.

"Yeah," Abby says. "You're nothing like Pete at all."

I can't think of anything to say, so I don't.

And Gordon says, "I doubt he ever expected us to escape the way we did. He wrote this letter to save face and make us feel helpless."

I don't say, "Maybe we are helpless."

What I do say is, "I'm gonna get some water."

Inside the kitchen, I:

    1. Refill my glass.

    2. Stare at the monsters on the fridge door.

    3. Fight back the memories flooding my mind.

Obviously, I know my friends can't see my past just by looking at me.

But still, I feel like hiding.

As soon as I hear footsteps on the tile:

    1. My heart hammers against my chest.

    2. Cicely's face flashes behind my eyes.

I turn around.

"You're really not like him, you know," Abby says. "You're nice, and caring, and you always look out for me. You make me feel like I have a brother again."

I:

    1. Didn't know I meant so much to her.

    2. Can't think of anything else to say but, "Thank you."

Abby smiles, and says, "I know you think it's dangerous for us to be close, but do you think we could hug, just this once?"

I nod.

We hug.

And Abby cries into my chest, over my heart.

"What's wrong?" I say, and I feel stupid for saying it.

Like Cicely said, everything's wrong.

Abby:

1. Steps back.

2. Wipes her nose on her sleeve.

3. Says, "I'm afraid Gordon's right, and you guys really did outsmart Pete in the cabin. What if he decides to kill us because we're not fulfilling his plans?"

"He won't," I say, and most of me believes it. "Pete called us some of his favorite projects. I'm sure he won't give up on abusing us so easily."

Of course, I'm also sure Pete won't want to torment us forever.

It's only a matter of time before he:

1. Tires of devouring our happiness.

2. Hungers for our lives.

But I don't tell Abby any of this.

Instead, I say, I try to believe, "Everything's gonna be alright. We'll find some way to stop Pete. We'll make him undo our curses."

"I don't care about that stuff," Abby says. "Maybe I'm evil for saying this, but I don't even care about getting my family back."

"You're not evil."

"I mean, I care about my family. I just don't know them. They're like shadows inside me, you know? But you and Cicely and everybody else, you're real. I don't know what I'd do without you."

"I understand. I'll do everything I can to stay alive."

"Thanks."

Abby and me, we:

1. Hug one more time.

2. Return to the living room.

And Ruth says, "I'd like to host a funeral for Kin at my house. That is, if you think Kin would approve."

"She would," Abby says. "She'd be really happy."

Ruth smiles a little. "Do you have any idea what kind of service she'd prefer?"

Abby nods. "She actually talked to me about that once. She said she wanted her funeral to be like a goodbye party. With streamers and cakes and stuff like that. She wanted us to celebrate her life, and life itself, you know?"

"Everything's going to hell," Cicely says, whispers.

In the silence that follows, my eyes search her face for the woman I knew.

I can't find her.

Then I:

    1. Put my hand on her arm.

    2. Say, "We'll be alright."

"I'm not just talking about us," Cicely says. "I'm talking about everyone. When I drop this ball, the world's going to end."

"We'll break the curse before that happens."

But Cicely doesn't seem to hear me. Or maybe she's ignoring me.

She:

    1. Frowns hard.

    2. Stares at the tennis ball, as if she can see the whole world collapsing on the yellow surface. Maybe she can.

"Cicely?" I say, trying to reach the woman I hope still exists inside her.

"I go there in my dreams," she says.

"Where?"

"The end of the world."

And I think:

    1. Meteor.

    2. Plague.

    3. Nuclear war.

Then Cicely says, "Every night, I open my eyes, and I'm at some location I've never been to before, and I can't move. I'm forced to watch as friends, or relatives, or lovers turn on each other. They scream and fight. The scenes usually end in murder. And afterward, I'm hit with a realization. This tragedy's going to happen because of me. Because when I drop this ball, all the respect remaining in the world will fade away."

"I'm sorry," I say. "Those sound like horrible nightmares."

"They're more than nightmares," she says, still staring at the ball. "They're visions. I've tried convincing myself that I'm only suffering a possible future, like in *A Christmas Carol*. But there's no preventing this hell. There's no stopping Pete." She laughs. "John used to say I had a difficult time facing reality, and now I know just how right he was. Somehow, I thought if I could just talk to Pete, face to face, we could come to some sort of agreement. But Pete's not going to compromise. Of course he's not. He's a psychopath."

Without another word, she:

    1. Stands up.

    2. Walks into her room.

    3. Closes the door.

My whole body shudders as Cicely's words eat away at something deep inside me.

Something precious.

Just as I make up my mind to go after Cicely, the bedroom door opens.

And I imagine her returning with a:

    1. Grin.

    2. Bizarre comment.

    3. Movie she wants us to watch.

Instead, she returns with a gun in her hand.

"What's going on?" I say.

"I'm sorry," Cicely says. "I can't do this anymore."

Her tone adds fuel to my terror, because she's never sounded so:

    1. Cold.

    2. Empty.

I stand up.

"Don't get any closer," Cicely says, pointing the gun at her head. "I have a few things I want to say, but if you try to stop me, I'll go right now."

I don't:

    1. Move.

2. Breathe.

Though I feel like screaming.

"This wasn't an easy decision," Cicely says. "You're all very special to me, and I hate to leave you like this. I wish there was more I could do for you."

"Please don't do this," Abby says, crying.

"I have to. I don't want to die, but more than that, I don't want to watch all the love in the world drain away. I don't want to become heartless."

"You won't, Cis. I promise. We'll find a way to keep that from happening."

"This is the only way."

In a heartbeat, the truth:

1. Consumes me.

2. Overpowers my fear.

Cicely's right.

So I say, "If you die, I'm dying with you."

"Hold on, Nick," Gordon says. "We don't even know if Cicely's right about the world ending. What if her curse is deluding her?"

"It doesn't matter. What matters is, without her, I'll have nothing left to live for." I look Cicely in the eyes. "I love you."

And for a few fleeting moments:

1. Cicely beams, bright.

2. The world is right in the living room again.

Then her smile withers away and she says, "I'm happy to hear that, hon. We can start a life together in the next world. Are you ready to pass on now?"

I nod.

"No!" Abby says, grabbing my arm. "You and Cis are like my family. You're all I have left. I need you."

"This doesn't have to be goodbye," I say.

"Nicholas is right," Cicely says, and points the gun at Abby. "You can come with us."

Abby:

1. Yelps.

2. Releases my arm.

3. Runs into her bedroom.

And Ruth:

    1. Slaps me, probably because I'm the one without the gun.

    2. Says, "Hasn't Abby suffered enough already?"

"We want to end her suffering," I say.

"Abby can join us when she's ready," Cicely says. "Shall we go, hon?"

I:

    1. Nod.

    2. Approach her.

"Do you want to go first?" Cicely says. "Or should I?"

"Either way," I say.

Then Ruth:

    1. Says, "Wait!"

    2. Picks up a pen from the coffee table.

    3. Writes on the back of an envelope.

"What are you doing?" I say.

Ruth:

    1. Doesn't respond.

    2. Writes for a while longer.

    3. Collapses on the couch.

Cicely and me, we rush over to her.

"Ruth?" Cicely says.

"What's going on?" Gordon says.

"Ruth's unconscious," I say. "She left us a note."

So out loud I read:

Dear Peons,

    I value our friendship, and so I've decided to save your pathetic little lives. I could, of course, use my powers to prevent you from killing yourselves, but then I'd have to put you on a 24/7 suicide watch. And that would get old fast. I have a life outside of work, and I need my me time.

I could also imbue your flesh with immortality, but let's face it. None of you deserve such a gift. Anyway, I don't want to run into you 1000 years from now, because that would be socially awkward for all of us.

And so I've decided to pencil in a meeting with you tomorrow. I'm sure we'll be able to work out an arrangement which will be mutually beneficial to all parties concerned. Therefore, it would be most imprudent of you to blow your bitty brains out at this time.

Yours faithfully,
Pete, Esq.

P.S. You're welcome.

#31

THERE ARE 3 ways I can see this ending:

1. Pete kills us.
2. Pete tortures us, then kills us.
3. Pete tortures us, lets us go, then torments us for days or weeks or years before deciding to finally finish us off.

I wish I could muster some hope for another conclusion:

4. Pete decides to let us live.

But I'm sure he won't limit how much he takes from us.

If my past has taught me anything, it's that a monster always wants more, because more is never enough.

Finally, Cicely stops convulsing.

"Are you awake?" I say.

"Yes," Cicely says, cold and empty, like the room.

"He hasn't shown himself yet."

"OK."

At this point, I want to:

1. Hold her.
2. Tell her everything's gonna be alright.

But instead, I:

1. Stay quiet.
2. Stare at the closed door.
3. Listen to the same throaty rumbling I heard the last time I was here.

After a while, Abby:

1. Stops trembling.

   2. Says, "What's going on?"

"Nothing yet," I say. "We're waiting for Pete."

"What do you think he's gonna do to us?"

"I don't know."

A moment later, the deep grumbling stops.

And I say, "I think he's coming."

Abby:

   1. Struggles against her leg shackles.

   2. Bursts into tears.

Then the door opens.

Pete:

   1. Emerges from the darkness.

   2. Smirks.

   3. Says, "Hiya, fellas."

Part of me regrets I didn't kill myself:

   1. Yesterday.

Or even:

   2. Years ago, when I took too many pills, and almost didn't call anyone.

The other part of me wants to:

   1. Become Batman.

   2. Battle my arch nemesis.

   3. Save the day.

But I do nothing.

As for Pete, he says, "I hope you're hungry, because I grilled us some Gordon and Ruth kabobs for lunch." He laughs. "No, your friends are fine. They may not be as important to me as the 3 of you, but they're still amusing enough not to slaughter. Anyway, I hate the taste of humans. No offense. Now, let's get down to brass tacks, shall we?"

No one replies.

I glance over at Cicely and notice her:

   1. Hands trembling.

   2. Eyes staring at the floor.

Pete recaptures my attention as he:

1. Approaches us, causing Abby to cry harder.
2. Stops right in front of Cicely.
3. Looks down at her, smiling.
4. Says, "You know, the first time I ever laid eyes on you, I didn't think much of your flesh. You're not exactly a traditional beauty, to say the least. But I have to admit, your body's grown on me. So much so, I've made a habit of smearing my presence all over you whenever you take a shower. It's one of the highlights of my day, actually."

Right now, I want to kick Pete in the balls.

But I just sit there.

And Pete says, "I want you to know, I'm not one of those people who only see women as sexual objects. Far from it. I'm interested in your mind, your emotions, the whole enchilada. Your suffering is a valuable asset to me, and I don't relish the thought of you finding a sort of nihilistic peace in oblivion. Therefore, after careful consideration, I've decided to lift your curse. I hope you understand how lucky you are. Normally, I wouldn't reverse any of my past achievements, but this is a special case. Your greatest pain is to witness the sorrow of others, and so even without your curse, I'm sure you'll live a long and entertaining life of misery with your friends."

I want to strangle Pete with my bare hands.

But I glance at my watch instead.

The face's cracked, and time's stopped.

And Pete says, "Before I act the hero and save the world, you need to give me a little tit for my tat. That's only fair. I want you to prove you're gonna be a loyal and obedient pet from now on. You have 5 minutes to convince me. So start begging, bitch."

At that, Cicely looks up at Pete with:

1. Fury in her forehead.
2. Grim passion in her eyes.

"No," she says, soft and strong, at the same time. "You're going to lift all our curses, and then you're going to release us."

Pete's smirk fades away.

And the relief I feel almost floods out of me in tears.

Maybe we won't survive this, but at least now I'm sure:

    1. Cicely's still Cicely.

    2. Yesterday was only an act.

At the time, of course, I wasn't 100% positive Cicely was still fighting for us.

But I hoped she was banking on the idea that Pete wouldn't want her to commit suicide.

Because he'd want to kill her himself.

So I decided to play along.

And I hoped Pete would be more willing to negotiate if 2 of us were ready to die.

Finally, Pete:

    1. Snaps out of his stasis.

    2. Smiles again.

    3. Says, "I hate to be a negative ninny, but I have to say, you're not off to a great start. You should consider taking off your top and licking the floor. Otherwise, you might run the risk of alienating your audience."

"I'm not going to demean myself for you," Cicely says.

"Yes, you will."

"I'm not your plaything, Peter."

And Pete:

    1. Says, "Yes, you are!"

    2. Points his finger at her face, as if he can destroy her with a single touch. Maybe he can.

Then she:

    1. Says, "It's over, hon."

    2. Reaches out.

He:

    1. Pulls his hand away.

    2. Takes a step back.

    3. Folds his arms over his chest.

4. Says, "Are you fucking crazy? Do you have any idea what I'm gonna do to you if you keep pissing me off?"

"Torture, murder," Cicely says. "Is that the long and short of it?"

"Yeah. The worst kind of torture imaginable. So if you value your life, you better start making me happy."

"I'm not responsible for your happiness, hon. But I am responsible for mine. And that means not putting up with your games anymore. I'd rather face the consequences of defying you."

"Then you really are nuts."

"Nuts or not, I'm tired of living my life in fear. You can abuse me, Peter. You can take your feelings out on me. But I'm not going to sacrifice my self for you anymore. And it's not just you I'm taking about, hon. Before you, there was John, and my ex-girlfriend Mary, and my parents. I've spent over 40 years of my life keeping constant vigilance over the real Cicely. Making sure she stayed buried deep inside. But she's risen from the dead now, and like most zombies, she's not going back in the ground without a fight. So you can either lift our curses and let us go, or you can kill me."

"Then I'll kill you."

Cicely sighs. "You remind me of my husband. At home, he spent most of his time trying to control me. And I usually let him. I'm sure he thought this power over me would make him happy, but it never did. He was a miserable man, just like you."

"I'm not a man."

"Whatever you are, I know you feel empty. I know you're trying desperately to fill that void, and I know you're not succeeding. The problem, hon, is that you're going about this the wrong way. But it's not too late. You can still turn your life around."

For a while, Pete:

1. Stares at Cicely in silence.
2. Bites his fingernails.

Then, he says, "You think you understand me, but you don't. You don't know what I am."

"It doesn't matter what you are," Cicely says.

"It fucking well does! I lost everything, and there's no getting it back. I've tried. This shadow of a life is all I have left."

At this point, Cicely:

1. Stands.

2. Looks at Pete, eye to eye.

3. Says, "I'll help you find more."

"You can't," he says, crackles.

"I will."

And maybe Pete's finally caught a glimpse of real power in her eyes.

Because he says, "OK."

Cicely:

1. Reaches out to touch his arm.

2. Passes right through him.

"I'm sorry, Ab," Pete says. "I don't think I can do this for you anymore."

I turn to Abby.

She:

1. Stares at the floor, blushing.

2. Says, "Oh no."

3. Closes her eyes. And the entire length of chain that runs from the wall, through our leg shackles, to a large ball, turns to dust.

4. Rushes to the stairs.

Cicely and me, we follow her.

"Wait!" Pete says. "You said you'd help me. Please."

"I'll stay with him," Cicely says.

And I say, "Are you sure?"

"Yes. I don't think he can hurt me. I don't think he ever could."

I feel:

1. Afraid about leaving her alone with this maniac.

2. A ferocious desire to confront Abby.

After a short struggle, my rage wins over.

"Don't hurt her," Cicely says.

And I:

    1. Say, "I won't." And whether I believe that or not, I don't care.

    2. Race up the stairs.

    3. Find myself in the kitchen of a normal-looking home.

    4. Follow the sound of crying into a windowless bedroom. Half the room's mostly pink, and the other half's mostly blue.

Abby's:

    1. On the bed.

    2. Curled up tight.

"Did you do it?" I say. "Did you curse us?"

Abby:

    1. Unfurls.

    2. Sits up.

    3. Wipes her eyes with her sleeve.

    4. Says, "I'm sorry."

And I realize Abby's:

    1. Not only sorry about the past 31 days.

    2. Apologizing for ruining my life.

The pain I feel, combined with all the other pain she's ever put me through, floods out of me in hatred.

So I:

    1. Jump on the bed.

    2. Push her back.

    3. Straddle her.

    4. Hold down her arms.

    5. Say, "You killed her, didn't you?"

"Who?" Abby says, crying.

"My mom. You killed her. Didn't you? Didn't you?!?"

And Abby:

    1. Looks away.

    2. Nods.

    3. Says, "I ate her."

Then I:

    1. Grip her throat with both hands, fast and easy.

    2. Squeeze.

Of course, it's not really Abby I'm attacking. I'm fighting the monster inside her, with the monster inside me.

She:

    1. Fights back.

    2. Gives me #31.

    3. Stops struggling.

    4. Stares at me.

And she's more than my enemy right now, even she doesn't know it. She's my true nature finally breaking free.

And deep down, in the darkness of my heart, I knew this time would come.

Because an asshole like me can't be restrained by:

    1. Lists.

    2. Numbers.

    3. Schedules.

Eventually, poof, that fairy tale world has come to an end.

So I keep squeezing Abby's neck.

And blame and fear swirl around inside me.

Blame because of:

    1. The things she's done.

    2. The secrets she's kept.

    3. The real Abby.

And fear because, if I don't kill her, she'll:

    1. Turn me into a rabbit and stomp me to death.

Or:

    2. Say that special word and kill me in an instant.

Or:

    3. Snap her fingers and zap me out of existence.

Tears fall onto Abby's face, and I:

    1. Can't stand looking at her anymore.

    2. Close my eyes.

And suddenly, I see Cicely.

She doesn't look at me:

    1. With I-don't-know-what's-got-into-you eyes.

    2. Like I'm a curse.

To her, there's something precious inside me.

Something good.

In the end, the love in my heart isn't strong enough to keep me from murdering Abby.

It's the respect that saves us.

And I:

    1. Say, "I'm sorry."

    2. Climb off of Abby.

    3. Say, "Are you dead?"

"I don't think so," Abby says.

Then, the light in the room dims.

Abby:

    1. Says, crackles, "Oh no."

    2. Rushes out of bed.

    3. Searches through a drawer in her nightstand.

"What's wrong?" I say.

"It's bedtime," Abby says. "I'm sorry, Nick. I don't remember where I put it."

"What are you talking about?"

"Keep away from her as long as you can."

"Who?"

Abby doesn't answer.

So I survey the room and notice:

    1. There's no lamp or other source of light, but the dim glow still exists.

    2. A white sheet stirring on the floor.

"Where did I put it?" Abby says.

Then the sheet:

    1. Begins to rise.

2. Forms a head at the apex.

"I found it!" Abby says.

And I jump.

This woman taking shape before me:

1. Points her arms me.

2. Wriggles her fingers.

3. Opens and closes her mouth.

"Drink this," Abby says, holding out a vial.

"What is it?" I say.

"It doesn't matter. If you don't drink it, the house will think you're an intruder. Hurry!"

Maybe Abby just wants to poison me.

But I:

1. Decide to trust the worry in her eyes.

2. Drink whatever's in the vial.

And the white sheet woman rushes at me.

I turn away from her to run, but she:

1. Wraps her arms around me, from behind.

2. Squeezes my arms and chest.

"Let him go!" Abby says. "He's Pete! Stop it!"

I:

1. Hear something inside me crack.

2. Feel hot air against the back of my neck.

Then the woman:

1. Loosens her embrace.

2. Says, whispers into my ear, "I love you."

3. Releases me.

I ease myself onto a pink chair, and watch as she:

1. Hugs Abby.

2. Returns to the corner of the room.

3. Collapses into a crumpled sheet on the floor.

"Are you alright?" Abby says.

"I think she broke a rib," I say.

And Abby:

    1. Says, "Oh no."

    2. Opens the drawer again.

    3. Removes some vials.

    4. Sets them on the nightstands.

"Who was that?" I say.

Abby:

    1. Says, "She wasn't anybody."

    2. Uses a dropper to drip a yellow liquid into a glass of water.

    3. Says, "She's just part of the house, you know?"

Obviously, I don't know, but I don't tell Abby that.

Instead, I say, "I'm sorry I almost killed you."

"That wasn't your fault," Abby says. "Our curses respond to each other, remember? They make you hurt me."

"So you really are cursed?"

"I lied about a lot of stuff, but not that."

Part of me wants to believe that I'm not responsible for my actions.

But still, I say, "The curses didn't make me choke you."

And Abby says, "But maybe they amplified your anger or something."

"Either way, I could've stopped myself before I hurt you. I'm sorry I didn't."

Abby:

    1. Hands me a cup of purple liquid.

    2. Says, "This should help with the pain and the healing."

Then I:

    1. Drink.

    2. Say, "You didn't really eat my mom, did you."

Abby shakes her head.

Maybe her curse forced her to lie about my mom, or maybe she just wanted to be punished. At this point, I don't really care the reason.

"But you did curse us," I say.

"Yeah," she says.

"Why?"

And while my bloodlust's gone, maybe I sound as furious as I feel.

Because Abby:

    1. Flinches.

    2. Sniffles.

    3. Sits on the bed.

    4. Picks at a scab on her ankle.

"Well?" I say.

"I don't know," Abby says. "I finally found a way out of the house, so I went to the grocery store. And I saw you and Cicely, and you both seemed so nice and funny. I liked you."

"So you decided to curse us?"

"Yeah."

I snicker, and a jagged pain explodes in my chest. "Why would you hurt people you like?"

"Because I'm not a good person, Nick."

"Why the tennis ball and the slapping?"

"I don't know. I cursed you, but I let your souls choose the manifestations."

"Would the world really end if Cicely dropped the ball?"

"I don't know that either. I mean, maybe she really does have the power to choose the fate of the world, and the curse exploited that. Or maybe Cis was being tricked."

"Is there anything you do know?"

Abby:

    1. Shrugs.

    2. Picks at her scab again.

And I stand up, slow and careful.

"What're you doing?" Abby says.

"I'm going back to the basement," I say. "I shouldn't've left Cicely alone with Pete."

"Cicely's fine. Trust me. Pete would never hurt anybody."

I almost laugh again. "You betrayed me, Abby. I can't trust you anymore."

"But Pete really didn't do anything. He talked to you in the basement today, and that time I brought you here. But I did everything else. Pete was just doing what I told him."

I:

    1. Head toward the door.

    2. Say, "Goodbye, Abby."

"Wait!" Abby says. "There's a barrier around the room. The same kind I put in the cabin, you know? There's no way to get out of here until morning."

"If you're so powerful, why don't you just remove the barrier?"

"I've tried, and I can't. I can get us out of the kitchen during the day, but my parents put a lot of themselves into this room. And they're stronger than me."

I'm almost positive Abby's lying to me again, so I reach for the doorknob.

"Don't!" Abby says.

But I do.

And the fear and the pain:

    1. Consume me.

    2. Overpower my desire to escape.

So I pull my hand away.

"Nick," Abby says, touching my back.

"Stay away from me!" I say.

Because I know Abby:

    1. Used reverse psychology to get me to touch the barrier.

    2. Feeds on my terror.

    3. Wants to devour me whole, once and for all.

"I'm not gonna hurt you," Abby says.

I run to the other side of the room.

And all I can do now is:

    1. Cry.

    2. Beg.

    3. Wait.

So I do.

But the inevitable doesn't happen.

Eventually, I:

    1. Feel somewhat secure again.

    2. Wipe away my tears.

Then the remaining light in the bedroom fades to pitch black.

"We have to get in bed," Abby says. "Hurry."

"I'm not getting in there with you," I say.

"You have to. Lights out is our last warning before we get punished. Please, Nick. I don't want you to get hurt again."

And I:

    1. Don't want to either.

    2. Head in the direction of the bed.

But I'm not going fast enough, apparently, because:

    1. My entire body itches with a dull pain.

    2. The voice of the sheet woman says, whispers, "Little boys who defy their parents burn in hell."

With every second, my agony intensifies.

I:

    1. Yelp as I climb onto the bed.

    2. Lie down.

    3. Tremble.

"I should've warned you sooner," Abby says. "I was thinking about other stuff, and I lost track of time. I'm so stupid."

"Is there anything else I need to do?"

"Just don't move. She'll do the rest."

So I lie still in the darkness as:

    1. A blanket lowers onto my body.

    2. The female presence tucks me in, tight.

    3. Cold lips press against my cheek.

"She'll leave us alone now," Abby says. "I mean, if we stay like this until morning."

"What about Cicely?" I say. "Is she safe?"

"Yeah. Eco won't hurt her unless she tries to come in here. And Pete'll explain that to her."

"We're not allowed to get out of bed?"

"No."

"What if I have to use the bathroom?"

"We have to go in here. I know that seems gross, but it won't leave a mess or anything. She always keeps everything nice and clean."

I shiver. "Who is she?"

"Like I said before, she's not really a person or anything. Eco's more like an idea. Like an expression of my parents' intentions, you know? They created her to take care of us when they weren't around. Me and Pete, I mean. He's my little brother."

"Oh. But why is she still around? You're both adults."

"Eco doesn't know that. My parents made her back when we were kids, and she still responds to stimuli the same way."

"Why haven't your parents deactivated her?"

Abby sighs. "They've been gone for a long time."

"I'm sorry."

"Don't be. They're horrible people. When they first created Eco, they only used her as a babysitter, you know? But then they started relying on her more and more, and they spent less and less time with us. One day, they left on one of their trips, and they never came back. Me and Pete were 6 and 8 then, I think."

Maybe Abby's only trying to win my sympathy by telling me a story I can relate to.

But I:

1. Give in to the heartbreak in my broken chest.
2. Say, "I'm sorry."

And Abby:

1. Weeps, soft.
2. Says, "I'm so pathetic. They abandoned us, and I'd still do anything to get them back."

"That's natural," I say. "I wish my mom would come home all the time."

"But it's different for you, Nick. You don't have any evidence that your mom hated you. Yeah, she disappeared and everything. But you don't know why. For all you know, she never wanted to go away."

"That didn't stop me from feeling abandoned, Abby."

"I'm not trying to minimalize your suffering or anything. I'm just saying I know my parents despise me. I know, because the night before they left us, I had this nightmare where the floor opened up and swallowed them. And when I woke up, I got out of bed, and I realized Eco wasn't active, because she didn't punish me, you know? So I went out to my parents' bedroom. Their door was locked, like always, so I just listened to them. They spent a while imprinting Eco with new commands, and then they said they'd go to a place where me and Pete could never find them. They didn't use our names though. Usually they called us Flotsam and Jetsam. It was like a joke to them. After that, Eco showed up and forced me back into bed. The next day, I convinced myself that everything I remembered from that night was just a bad dream. And I held on to that lie for a long time. It was only a couple years ago that I really accepted the truth. And now I know for sure they don't love me. But I don't know how to stop loving them. So I really am pathetic."

And I can't think of anything else to say but, "I'm sorry."

Abby cries again.

Then I

1. Do think of something else to say.
2. Say, "You're not pathetic. You're just a human being in a messed up world. I mean, if you are human. Are you human?"

"I think so," Abby says.

I:

1. Consider holding her hand.
2. Wonder if Eco would allow that.
3. Don't move.
4. Think about Abby's story.
5. Feel uncomfortable about how much I understand her.

And suddenly, the chaos of the last 31 days makes a strange sort of sense to me.

Abby didn't just want Cicely and me to suffer.

She wanted to:

1. Suffer with us.

2. Bond through a common torment, the way she probably did with Pete. Or the way I did with Karl, years ago. So she cursed us. I'm not sure how Abby knew Cicely and me would tell each other about our problems, but maybe she didn't know. Maybe she only hoped. And after Cicely posted those flyers around town, Abby made contact and joined our group. Maybe Abby expected Cicely to reach out to other cursed individuals, or maybe she just jumped on the opportunity to respond to the flyer, because this approach was less suspicious than her original infiltration plan. Of course, Abby could tell me which of these scenarios is true, but I don't care enough to ask.

3. Isolate us from the rest of the world. So she made those nasty calls to our families and friends, using our voices.

4. Keep us from discovering the truth. So she kidnapped me, and Pete pretended to be the perpetrator, and he threatened to erase Cicely from existence if we tried to find him. I'm sure Abby thought we'd find her out if we kept searching and investigating long enough. Maybe we would've.

5. Fulfill her longing for physical attention, however possible. So she took us to the cabin and supplied a list of twisted tasks we were supposed to perform in order to escape.

In other words, Abby and me are kindred spirits.

And I know the worst part isn't that she feels:

1. Naked.

2. Empty.

3. Alone.

The real curse is that she believes:

1. This void inside her is all she deserves.

2. Without manipulation and coercion, no one would ever choose to get close to her.

And I feel sorry for:

1. Abby.

But also:

2. Myself.

"Are you asleep?" Abby says.

"Just thinking," I say. "And I think I understand what you were after by using us. But why did you target Cicely and me when you already have people in your life? Why didn't you curse them?"

"You mean Pete?"

"Pete and Kin."

"I wanted to spend some time with nice people, so that ruled Pete out. He used to be my best friend, but he's been pretty mean to me ever since he died."

"I'm sorry. I didn't know he wasn't alive."

"Yeah, we do a good job at making him look solid." Abby sighs. "I'm so stupid. I thought if he looked alive and acted alive, he might start feeling like his old self again, you know? I thought if we worked together on a project, we might get back some of what we lost. But things've only gotten worse. He spends most of his time in our parents' room, watching TV, and he barely talks to me. When he does, he just tells me what to do or says what I'm doing wrong. I know I should spend more time trying to help him, but most of the time I can't stand looking at him. I'm a horrible sister."

"I don't think that's true."

Abby sighs. "You're just saying that because you don't know me that well. It's my fault Pete died. I could've stopped him, but I didn't. When he was alive, he was a really angry person. He hated my parents and eventually he started taking out his feelings on the house. I knew that defying Eco was dangerous for his body and his soul, but I never tried to stop him, because I liked seeing someone stand up to her. One day, Pete refused to brush his teeth, and Eco tried to force him. He struggled around so much that she accidentally forced the toothbrush into his brain. I mean, I think it was an accident. But either way, I could've prevented it. I let him die."

"You're not responsible for what happened."

"That's nice of you to say, Nick, but I know better. I'm not the naïve little woman I pretend to be."

"I don't think you're naïve, Abby. I think you're harder on yourself than you should be."

"That's not true. I don't even hate myself for what I did to you and Cicely. I'm just glad I got to spend some time with you guys."

"I still think you should stop blaming yourself for what happened to Pete."

"Then we'll have to agree to disagree."

I:

    1. Want to save her from her guilt.

    2. Can't even save myself.

"Anyway," Abby says. "You were wondering about Kin too. The reason why I didn't curse her is because she's not real."

"What do you mean?" I say.

"I made you believe Kin was erased from reality and Ruth was one of Pete's creations, but Kin never existed in the first place. Ruth was always the real one. She's a neighbor of mine, and I kidnapped her and brought her here, and filled her with my intentions. Like how my parents imprinted Eco, you know? I put an imaginary person inside her."

And suddenly, I remember how Ruth:

    1. Recovered memories of being Kin.

    2. Remembered lying on a couch as Abby read to her from a book.

So this was probably the imprinting process.

And I remember how Kin:

    1. Performed a psychic reading.

    2. Advised that we stop trying to find the one who cursed us.

So this was another one of Abby's attempts to keep us off her trail.

"You used her like a puppet," I say.

"Yeah," Abby says. "I considered keeping her like that forever. I even thought about controlling you and Cicely that way. But I decided I wanted something more than that. Something more real."

"I see."

And I:

    1. Think about Abby's abilities and powers.

2. Feel helpless.

3. Wonder if I'm going to survive.

Then Abby says, "I know this doesn't make what I did right or anything, but I want you to know, I wasn't gonna keep you guys cursed for long. You'll go back to normal as soon as I die, and I'm gonna die really soon."

I imagine Abby taking too many pills, the way I did, years ago.

"I'm not gonna kill myself or anything," Abby says, like she read my mind. Maybe she did. "The world's gonna keep attacking me until I'm dead."

And I:

1. Say, "Who did this to you?"

2. Think of her parents.

Then Abby says, "I manipulated the energies in order to hurt people, and my wounds are the consequence. I've done a lot of bad stuff, so it's only a matter of time before it all catches up with me."

Once again I feel:

1. A strong desire to comfort her.

2. Afraid that she's trying to deceive me again.

But then I:

1. Remember when Abby described the funeral she said Kin wanted, with streamers and cake.

2. Realize Abby probably wanted this goodbye party for herself.

"Maybe you'll survive the curse," I say.

"I won't," Abby says. "I'm really connected with the energies and everything, and I can feel the world's anger closing in on me."

"I've felt that way before, Abby. And I don't think that feeling has anything to do with curses."

"No offense, but I'm talking about forces that you don't understand."

And maybe Abby's right.

Or maybe this has:

1. Nothing to do with the Universe or God.

2. Everything to do with the road to redemption Abby's constructed in her mind.

So I say, "I don't doubt that you cursed yourself by hurting us, but maybe you're the one attaching blame to these consequences. Maybe you're not being punished. Maybe you can give yourself another chance."

"Life doesn't work that way, Nick."

"You don't know that. Maybe if you start doing good in the world, your curse will break."

"That would never happen."

"It's worth a try, isn't it?"

"I don't want to talk about this anymore."

"Alright."

"I think I'm ready for sleep."

"Alright."

After a long silence, Abby says, "Nick?"

"Yeah?"

"You drank part of Pete's corpse, so now Eco thinks you're him. And I keep thinking about how you couldn't escape the house unless I broke you out. I could let you stay trapped here, like Pete used to be, and you could keep me company until I die. Then you could read through the books my parents left behind, and eventually you'd become powerful enough to create a gateway. But I decided I'm not gonna make you do that. I'm gonna let you go."

And I can't think of anything else to say but, "Thank you."

#32

ECO WON'T GIVE Abby and me any free time until after we:

1. Take a bath.
2. Brush our teeth.
3. Comb our hair.
4. Change into clean clothes.
5. Eat a non-vegan breakfast.

So we do.

Then I:

1. Follow Abby into her parents' bedroom.
2. See Pete with his legs inside a generator. And this must be the rumbling I heard from the basement before.
3. Notice the exhaust funneling into a point near the dresser, and disappearing.
4. Beam.
5. Hug Cicely.
6. Say, "Are you alright?"

"Fine and dandy," Cicely says. "Like a unicorn on a rainy day."

"Unicorns like rain?"

"Not especially, but they consider rainbows a delicacy."

"Oh."

"Are you OK?"

"I am now."

Pete:

1. Steps out of the generator.

2. Says, "You can turn this thing off now."

Cicely turns off the machine.

And Abby says, "Are you sure you don't want more? I can barely see you."

Pete:

1. Drifts closer to Abby.

2. Says, "I only wanted enough juice so I could talk to you before I pass over."

"You can't!" Abby says. "You'll go to hell."

"Cicely thinks hell's just another idea our parents put into Eco to control us. And I think she's right."

"But what if you're wrong?"

"Then I'll spend eternity getting tortured or living alone in some void. And of course I'm terrified of those possibilities, but I'm willing to take the chance. I've decided to trust there's something better waiting for me on the other side."

Then Abby:

1. Cries.

2. Says, crackles, "Please, Pete. I don't want you to go."

"I know, Ab," Pete says. "But Cicely's right. This place isn't good for me. I was getting off on playing the psychopath, and I think I'm starting to become one."

"That's not true. You're a good person."

Pete laughs. "How can you say that after how I've treated you?"

"You only treated me that way because I killed you."

"What are you talking about? Eco killed me. Our parents killed me."

"If I tried breaking out of the house sooner, we could've escaped, and you'd still be alive. But I liked being trapped here with you. I knew how much the house bothered you and hurt you, but I didn't care. You're right to hate me."

"I don't hate you, Ab. I'm just a bitter asshole of a phantom. Being near you reminded me of everything I lost, so I avoided you as much as possible. It's not your fault I couldn't cope with being dead, and it's not your fault I died."

"But I—"

"I don't have much time left." And he sounds muted, like he's speaking from somewhere far away. Maybe he is. "I want you to know that I love you and

I didn't mean…"

At this point, I can't see or hear Pete anymore.

And Abby:

1. Stares at the spot where Pete was floating.

2. Says, whispers, "Come back."

He doesn't.

"I'm sorry, hon," Cicely says. "I'm sure he's in a better place now."

Then Abby:

1. Glares at Cicely.

2. Looks at the floor.

3. Bites her fingernails.

4. Says, "I'll open a gateway for you guys."

5. Walks out of the bedroom.

Cicely and me, we follow.

And in the kitchen, Abby:

1. Presses her hands against the back door for a few minutes.

2. Trembles.

3. Weeps, soft.

4. Opens the door.

5. Says, "You better go before it closes."

Cicely:

1. Touches Abby's arm.

2. Says, "Come with us."

Then Abby:

1. Steps away from Cicely.

2. Leans against the wall.

3. Says, "I know what you want, and you don't have to worry. I'll unravel your curses soon. I can do it from here. I just need a few hours to prepare everything."

"I appreciate that, hon," Cicely says. "But I'd still like you to come with us. You need help."

"I don't need anything anymore."

"Please, Abby. You don't belong here."

"This is my home. This is the only place I do belong."

"I can help you."

"Like you helped Pete? I don't want to see you ever again, Cicely. You sent Pete to hell, and I could steal Nick to replace him, and I told Nick I wasn't gonna do that. But if you don't leave right now, I might change my mind."

So Cicely and me, we:

    1. Walk through the threshold.

    2. Turn around.

And Abby says, "Don't bother coming back. I'm gonna put up a barrier so strong, nobody could ever break through."

Then the door slams shut.

And I wonder if the chaos of the last 32 days is finally over.

Maybe Abby will keep her word.

Or maybe she'll:

    1. Never remove our curses.

    2. Kidnap me.

    3. Treat me like a puppet.

    4. Imprison me for years.

But I decide to hope for a happy ending anyway.

Outside of the nightmare created by Abby's parents, I escape to Sol's house. In this house, there's:

    1. No alcohol.

    2. No swearing.

    3. No surprises. Usually.

Sol:

    1. Hugs me, tight.

    2. Says, "My son, my son."

"Hi, Dad," I say.

"Let's sit down before I collapse, hm? My new exercise routine is a killer."

I nod.

We sit on the couch.

And Sol says, "Before you tell me what you came here to tell me, I want you to know that I'll always love you. I'll love you no matter what. Even if you've started drinking again."

"I haven't," I say.

"OK."

"I want to talk about Mom."

Sol doesn't speak for a few heartbeats. "You do?"

"Yeah."

Sol:

    1. Rubs his legs.

    2. Says, "I miss her."

And I:

    1. Feel tiny flames all over my body.

    2. Say, "Me too."

"She was a good woman," Sol says.

"Yeah."

"I didn't appreciate her enough when she was with us."

"I didn't either."

Sol:

    1. Looks at me for a long while.

    2. Shudders.

    3. Closes his eyes.

    4. Covers his face with his hands.

    5. Cries.

    6. Says, "I'm sorry, Nicholas. I did everything wrong."

"What do you mean?" I say.

Sol stares at his hands. "I did everything wrong when your mother died. That's why you started drinking, and that's why you tried to kill yourself. I've always tried denying that to myself, but it's true. I hurt you so deeply."

"You never hurt me, Dad."

"I did, Nicholas. Whenever you spoke about your mother, I reminded you that she would return to us someday. I thought I was doing the right thing by keeping our hope alive. But all I did was keep you from grieving."

"You didn't stop me, Dad."

"But you felt alone because of me. You were alone. I lived in my fantasies, and I did everything I could to talk you out of feeling your sadness, because I didn't want to feel my own. I betrayed you, because I didn't want to accept the truth."

"I wanted to believe she was coming back just as much as you did."

"I should have given her a funeral."

"We don't know what happened to her. She could still be alive."

"If she is alive, then I'm sure she left because of me. I was a terrible husband."

"That's not true."

"I didn't spend enough time with her. I was obsessed with my job."

I wipe my eyes. "Stop blaming yourself, Dad."

"I barely knew her, Nicholas."

"Even if you two had problems, she didn't have to leave you. You could've worked things out a different way, but she didn't give you the chance. That's not your fault."

Sol takes a deep breath. "Maybe you're right. Maybe you're right."

I study my broken watch.

"Do you need to be somewhere?" Sol says.

And I:

    1. Say, "No."

    2. Look at Sol for a long while.

    3. Say, "Sometimes I wish Mom were dead."

"What?" Sol says. "Why?"

"If she were dead, then maybe she loved me."

"Why do you say that? Of course she loved you."

"But if she's alive, then she really did abandon me. And I don't think a mother who loved her son would do that. So sometimes part of me wishes she were dead."

Sol:

    1. Holds my hands.

   2. Says, "Nicholas, she loved you with all her heart."

And I:

   1. Feel my eyes watering.

   2. Shake my head.

   3. Say, "There's no way Mom could've abandoned me and loved me. Those contradict each other."

"You mother loved you," Sol says. "She was a passionate woman. A very passionate woman. I never knew what she was thinking, but I always knew how she was feeling. She adored you, son. I promise you that."

And maybe he's only trying to make me feel better.

But I decide to trust him, fully, like a child.

Sol:

   1. Squeezes my hands.

   2. Says, "I've never told anyone this. Not even Brienda. But I used to imagine your mother talking to me."

"Yeah?" I say.

And Sol:

   1. Looks at the last photograph of my mom in the house.

   2. Says, "She would tell me that she was safe. And that she would come back to us someday, and we would become a family again. I would apologize for every terrible thing I did to her, and she forgave me. She hasn't spoken to me for years, but now she's telling me something new."

My heart beats fast, as if my mother's going to speak to me from my father's mouth. Maybe she will.

"She says she loves us," Sol says. "And she wants us to be happy. And I don't know if you know this, but your mother wasn't treated very well by your grandmother. Your mother says that she left us because she was afraid of hurting us the same way. Your mother knows that this was a terrible reason to abandon us, and she regrets doing it. But at the time, she didn't know how else to protect us."

"Oh," I say.

And this story is far from the fairy tales I imagined as a child.

But maybe it's enough.

#127

AFTER CICELY DROPS the tennis ball, the world as we know it comes to an end.

She:

    1. Divorces John.

    2. Quits her job.

    3. Moves to the mountains.

And in this dream home, Cicely's my girlfriend. I try to open up and tell her how I feel, even when I want to hide under our pastel bed, and she always listens. She never ignores me.

Tonight, I try to repay her kindness with some of my own.

"What's this?" Cicely says.

"A present," I say.

"Is it a pygmy chimera?"

"You'll see."

She opens the box. "Wow!"

"Is that a happy wow?"

"Are there unhappy wows?"

"I think so."

"Well, this is definitely a happy wow. I love him. He looks just like you."

"I wanted to make you something that symbolizes how much I trust you, so I thought, what about a voodoo doll? Now you can hurt me whenever you want, but I know you won't. You'd never hurt me on purpose." I sigh. "Is this romantic or just creepy?"

"A little of both. But that's not a bad thing. Thank you, Nicholas."

And we kiss.

Then Cicely says, "Now shall we go have that talk with the cat?"

I:

    1. Nod.

    2. Say, "Do you think we're doing the right thing?"

"I hope so," Cicely says.

We head into the living room and find the cat:

    1. Sitting on her spot on the couch.

    2. Licking her leg.

"Abby," Cicely says.

And the cat:

    1. Glances at us.

    2. Goes back to cleaning herself.

"You can stop pretending," I say. "We know it's you."

I'm lying, of course, but the evidence does point in that direction.

    1. The cat showed up at our cabin a few weeks ago, and she didn't have any tags. And judging by Abby's past behaviors, she wouldn't hesitate to exploit our compassion in this way.

    2. I've known friendly and affectionate cats, but she's far beyond the norm. She hardly spends any time alone.

    3. She's accident-prone.

"I know you're not trying to hurt us," Cicely says. "But you are. You can't keep lying to us, hon."

The cat:

    1. Turns around 2 times.

    2. Curls up.

    3. Closes her eyes.

And Cicely says, soft and strong, "Nicholas and I care about you, Abby, so we're giving you one more chance. You have to leave now, but you can come back if you come back as Abby. If you try to deceive us again, we won't open our home to you anymore."

The cat doesn't move.

Cicely:

    1. Picks up the cat.

    2. Carries her out the front door.

    3. Sets her down.

    4. Says, "Goodbye, Abby."

The cat:

    1. Looks up at us.

    2. Turns around.

    3. Walks away.

Cicely and me, we watch the cat fade into the dark frost.

Then we sit on the couch.

"Do you think she'll come back?" I say.

"I don't know," Cicely says, and she sounds a little sad. "Well, I think it's about time I paint a head on my Vaudevillian snapping turtle."

"Alright," I say.

So Cicely works on her new mural.

And I head into the bedroom.

Sure, I don't create as many lists as I used to, but I still write in my little purple notebook every night.

I write about how Cicely:

    1. Names my moles after B-movie directors.

    2. Compliments the trees when we go for hikes.

    3. Makes winter coats for her yard gnomes.

    4. Calls Ruth every week, and listens to her problems.

    5. Puts on elaborate puppet shows for the neighborhood kids.

    6. Makes a special meal for Meta, whenever she and Gordon visit.

    7. Kisses me on the cheek every night before bed. According to her, this is to make up for all the slapping.

Tonight, she gives me #127.

And she's more than my girlfriend right now, even if she doesn't know it. She's my redemption.

Of course, part of me still feels like I'm:

    1. Stupid.

2. Pathetic.

3. The same asshole I always was.

And sometimes I feel like I don't deserve Cicely.

But at this point, I don't care.

Because the other part of me is the Batman of Love.

And if the meaning of life is to get so wrapped up in living that you don't care about the meaning anymore, then I must be doing something right.

About the Author

Jeremy C. Shipp's work has appeared or is forthcoming in over 50 publications, the likes of *Cemetery Dance*, *ChiZine*, *Apex Magazine*, *Pseudopod*, and *The Magazine of Bizarro Fiction*. While preparing for the collapse of civilization, Jeremy enjoys living in Southern California in a moderately haunted Victorian farmhouse with his wife, Lisa, and their legion of yard gnomes. His other books include *Vacation* and *Sheep and Wolves*. And thankfully, only one mime was killed during the making of his first short film, *Egg*. Feel free to visit his online home at www.jeremycshipp.com, but beware the spork-wielding jerboa ninjas.

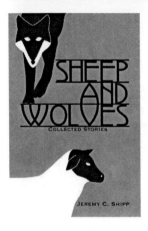

Breinigsville, PA USA
18 August 2010
243815BV00002B/198/P